721 SECRETS

*Keeping you up to date on all that goes on
at Manhattan's most elite address!*

Americans expect monarchs to be starched and stodgy—Caspia's crown prince Sebastian Stone is anything but. The part-time resident of apartment 12B is a knockout with onyx eyes and a chiseled chest. And he likes to show off that great bod! Just ask the multitude of women he's left in his wake. Or ask Tessa Banks, his lucky midtown assistant. Even in her tailored business suits, Tessa has been known to drool after her royal boss. But who could blame her? The sexy prince was sorely missed at the building's recent landmark party. Rumor has it he has taken his lowly secretary to his homeland palace. They've been spotted tête-à-tête at numerous Caspian locations—and *not* over business. How did a middle-class manager like Tessa morph into Cinderella anyway? We'd love to know her secret! Meanwhile let's hope Tessa can handle the smooth moves of the legendary lothario. The prince-we-pant-over is due back to 721 any day. Only then can we sort out super-sexy fact from ultra-sexy fiction....

Dear Reader,

I grew up surrounded by old hand-colored editions of fairy tales that had belonged to my mother and her mother and probably her mother, too. When the editors at Silhouette Books asked me to write this story for the PARK AVENUE SCANDALS series, I jumped at the chance to create a prince from an exotic faraway country.

While some of the story takes place in the New York City area where I live with my own handsome prince, I had a great time inventing Prince Sebastian's homeland of Caspia. I think everyone should have a chance to create a country. What would you like to see in yours? Mine has warm sunny weather (with no humidity!), calm blue seas, rugged terrain for hiking, striking classical architecture and delicious Mediterranean food.

By the time I'd finished writing I was sure the ancient and picturesque nation of Caspia could be found on a map somewhere between Italy and Greece. I was also ready to book a trip there as soon as possible.

I hope you enjoy your journey to Caspia with Sebastian and Tessa.

Jennifer Lewis

JENNIFER LEWIS

PRINCE OF MIDTOWN

Published by Silhouette Books
America's Publisher of Contemporary Romance

To the editors at Silhouette Desire who've encouraged me and supported my books, including senior editor Melissa Jeglinski, my first editor Demetria Lucas and my current editor Diana Ventimiglia. Big thanks to the people who read this book while I was writing it, including Amanda, Anne, Anne-Marie, Betty, Carol, Cynthia, Leeanne, Marie and Mel, and my agent Andrea. Once again I am indebted to Amanda and Carol for their business expertise. Special thanks and acknowledgment to Jennifer Lewis for her contribution to the PARK AVENUE SCANDALS miniseries.

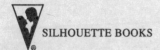 SILHOUETTE BOOKS

ISBN-13: 978-0-373-76891-2
ISBN-10:   0-373-76891-5

PRINCE OF MIDTOWN

Visit Silhouette Books at www.eHarlequin.com

Printed in U.S.A.

Books by Jennifer Lewis

Silhouette Desire

The Boss's Demand #1812
Seduced for the Inheritance #1830
Black Sheep Billionaire #1847
Prince of Midtown #1891

JENNIFER LEWIS

has been dreaming up stories for as long as she can remember and is thrilled to be able to share them with readers. She has lived on both sides of the Atlantic, and she worked in media and the arts before growing bold enough to put pen to paper. Jennifer is happily settled in New York with her family, and she would love to hear from readers at jen@jen-lewis.com.

Who's Who at 721 Park Avenue

6A: Marie Endicott—Suicide or murder? The investigation continues.

9B: Amanda Crawford—The cheerful event planner has a few secrets of her own.

9B: Julia Prentice—The society girl has gotten married to the infamous Wall Street millionaire Max Rolland…and there's a baby on the way.

12A: Vivian Vannick-Smythe—The building's longest-standing resident who has been on edge lately. Could it be planning the celebration of the building's landmark status, or something else?

12B: Prince Sebastian of Caspia—The eligible royal is back in Manhattan…and seducing his social secretary!

12C: Trent Tanford—The building's playboy seems to have finally settled down.

Penthouse A: Reed and Elizabeth Wellington—Happily married or happily fooling themselves?

Penthouse B: Gage Lattimer—The mysterious billionaire continues to be an enigma.

One

"You can't leave."

Sebastian Stone, Crown Prince of Caspia, spoke with such authority and conviction that for a moment Tessa Banks actually believed him.

Her boss's hard, handsome features seemed taut with stronger emotion than usual. He shoved a hand through his black hair and rose from the wide antique desk in his Midtown Manhattan office.

Tessa's stomach contracted with anxiety—and with the infuriating heat of arousal he always stirred in her.

Hang tough. This is your life.

She took a deep breath. "I've been your personal assistant for almost five years. I appreciate the freedom and responsibility you've entrusted me with, but it's time for me to move on."

"Move on?" He blew out an exasperated breath. "This

is not a gypsy caravan. It's a business. I'm counting on you to help me sort out this mess that's been dumped in my lap."

Tessa resisted the urge to point out that Caspia Designs might well have more in common with a gypsy caravan than an actual business. The conglomerate of luxury brands was colorful, extravagant and weighted with tradition. A crystal ball might reveal more lucid information than accounting ledgers that could only be described as "creative."

It was obvious, however, that her boss was not in a joking mood.

He strode across the office and grabbed the pile of papers from his in-box. "Please schedule a meeting tomorrow morning with Reed Wellington. I wish to consult him about my plans for Caspia Designs." He paused and flicked through the mail, a frown on his majestic brow. "And you must find me a new house sitter."

What? Did he plan to simply ignore her resignation?

Tessa's skin prickled with a combination of fury and desperation as she stood in speechless silence.

Her boss shook his head as he studied one paper. Accounts receivable, probably. It wasn't a pretty sight.

She wished she wasn't leaving at a time when Sebastian needed help pulling Caspia Designs together. He'd been handed the reins of the once-prestigious company by his father, the king, only to discover it was in a shambles.

But if this was how little concern he showed for *her* needs, she should be glad to leave him in the lurch.

Things must be serious, though. For one thing, he was wearing a suit. Usually his broad chest bore the insignia of whatever luxury brand he'd most recently convinced to open a boutique in his beloved Caspia. Fendi, Prada, Gucci—if there was a T-shirt with the logo on it, Sebastian cheerfully wore it to celebrate the new partnership.

Today fine gray wool draped his powerful physique. She should heave a sigh of relief that at least she didn't have to tear her gaze from his impressive biceps.

Right now she was too damn angry to care.

She laid her company PDA on the desk. "I'm moving to California in two weeks. If you prefer, I can leave immediately."

Sebastian muttered a curse, but still didn't look up. He flipped over a page of the report she'd put together and traced a column of numbers with a sturdy finger.

Tessa blinked, struggling to keep her breathing under control.

After all this time she was another office fixture, like the Aeron chair, the platinum penholder or the rack of servers. A simple, functional object without a will of its own.

"Goodbye." Her voice shook as she took a step toward the door. She had to climb over one of the cardboard crates of dusty papers that had consumed most of this last month, including three solid weekends. She'd given enough of her life in service to the Crown of Caspia.

"Where are you going?"

Sebastian's voice rattled the antique floor-to-ceiling windows that flooded the nineteenth-century brownstone with light.

"If you'd cared enough to listen, you'd know I'm leaving for California!" She'd never raised her voice to him before.

Sebastian put the file on the leather surface of the desk. "Tessa, you can't be serious?"

"Why not?" She wished her voice didn't sound so whiny and uncertain.

"Because I *need* you."

Spoken in his deep voice, the words echoed through her.

She steadied herself with a hand on the door frame.

If only he did need *her,* not just a faceless assistant who took care of everything so efficiently that she rendered herself invisible.

But he didn't. He had celebutantes and supermodels and starlets from Hollywood to Bollywood hurling themselves at him every minute of the day.

She should know. She fielded their calls.

"Tessa." He stepped toward her, skillfully negotiating an open box of papers. "You do realize I'd be lost without you."

His eyes fixed on hers with penetrating intensity. Large, dark and slightly almond shaped, those eyes had the power to make her do almost anything.

Her toes curled inside her shoes.

He's just saying it to stop you from leaving him in the lurch.

Still…

She lifted her chin. "I'm turning thirty in a month." She hesitated. Her personal life wasn't his business.

"What does that have to do with anything?"

Typical. Why would he care that she wanted a husband children, a real life?

No need to mention that, she told herself. Better t leave with a shred of dignity. "It's time for a change."

"Tessa." He crossed his arms and stared at her. "If yo were dissatisfied with your position in any way, you shoul have come to me immediately. Is it your job title? Your salary? We'll change them right now."

"It's neither of those things."

She hesitated, anxious not to reveal that *he* was part of the reason she needed to leave.

Sebastian Stone, christened The Prince of Midtown by the New York tabloids who tracked his every bold move, was a constant reminder of everything she was missing.

Especially since he barely knew she was alive.

"I feel as if I'm stuck in a rut. My life is slipping through my fingers…" Could she come up with anything that wasn't a soggy cliché?

"And California is the golden land of opportunity?"

"I know it isn't, but I need to shake things up." She shrank from his forceful black gaze and paced across the room. Her heart hammered beneath her designer dress.

"What's the job you've been offered?"

She shoved her hair behind her ear. "I don't have a job lined up yet. I'm sure I can find one when I get there."

"Then why California? You're not running off after some man, are you?"

Tessa froze. Her stomach lurched. "There is someone, yes."

Sebastian hesitated. An unfamiliar sensation crept over him. "I didn't know you were seeing someone."

"Well." Tessa blinked. "You're my boss."

"But we're friends, too, are we not? You could have told me you were being swept off your feet and were preparing to run away and desert me."

"You've been in Caspia for the last three months. I haven't seen you."

True.

"And it's not as if he's asked me to marry him or anything, so there wasn't that much to tell." She shoved a hand into her hair. Long, golden hair. Rumpled, as if she'd been running her fingers through it all day.

Unexpected desire mingled with the irritation in his blood. "So he's asked you to move clear across the country for him, but he's not even proposed to you?"

Her high-boned cheeks colored. "No. It's not like that."

"Who is this man?"

Tessa blew out a breath. "His name's Patrick Ramsay. He's a lawyer." She picked up a paperweight off the desk and held it poised in her elegant fingers. "We've been seeing each other for a few months. He's joining a practice in L.A. and, two days ago, he asked me if I'd like to move there with him."

"And you said yes?" Disbelief and indignation made him splutter.

She spun on her long, slender legs and strode across the room. "I told him I had to think about it. Now I've thought about it." She kept her face turned away from him. "And I've decided it's just the change I need."

"You're wrong." He'd never been so sure of anything.

She turned to face him, her green eyes wide. "I feel bad leaving, especially now that you've taken over Caspia Designs. I know there's a lot of work to do. But what if this is my one chance?"

Her voice rose to a high note that tugged at something in his chest. How could such a beautiful and talented woman be willing to throw her whole life away on a gamble?

"The name Patrick Ramsay rings a bell." An alarm bell.

"He's quite well known. He represented Elaina Ivanovic in her divorce from her husband Igor."

Sebastian's hackles shot up. "The *divorce* lawyer?" He'd seen that smarmy hustler on TV. Patrick Ramsay didn't know the meaning of the term *low blow.*

She nodded, jerked her imploring gaze from him and started across the far end of the room. "He's very nice, really. Busy, as you'd expect, but kind and thoughtful and— Oh!"

She tripped on an open box and sprawled forward. Adrenaline surged through Sebastian and he leaped across the room. "Are you hurt?"

"No! I'm fine. How silly of me." She blushed charmingly as he helped her up, her hand hot inside his.

On her feet, she pushed her hair back. "It's my fault for leaving these boxes everywhere. I'll stack them against the wall before I go."

"You'll do no such thing." He still held her hand. He didn't want to let go of it. To let go of Tessa.

She was the best assistant he'd ever had. Since he now spent most of his time in Europe, he needed someone he could count on to show up for work even with no one else there. Tessa had proven herself a sharp-minded self-starter and—until now—as steadfast as the rocks in the ancient harbor at Caspia.

He trusted her with everything, from his personal affairs to the embarrassing state of Caspia Designs's financials.

She tried to pull her hand back. He held it fast.

"Tessa, you are indispensable to me. What can I say that will make you stay?"

Her gaze skittered over his face and he sensed the swell of her emotion. Her muscles tensed, as if she wanted to say something but couldn't form the words.

Why had he never noticed how mobile and expressive her mouth was? Or that her skin had an iridescent sheen, like a haze of gold dust?

In that moment of contemplation she jerked back and tugged her hand from his grasp. Cool air assaulted his palm.

She turned and strode away, her slim body held stiff. "I don't want anything."

"I do."

The words fell from his lips before he'd formulated the thoughts to go along with them.

It pained him to see her pacing the floor like a nervous colt, ready to gallop off to disaster.

She belonged here, with him.

His own conviction surprised him. Was some primal masculine jealousy aroused by the thought of her with another man?

Possibly.

She bent over a box filled with hanging files. Her back strained under the weight as she tried to lift it.

"Put that down." He marched over, hefted the box off the floor and shoved it against the wall. The exertion felt good. Then he heaved another into position next to it. He glanced at Tessa. "I don't want you injuring yourself."

A brow shot up and her green eyes flashed. "I may be skinny, but I'm strong."

She picked up a box, dumped it next to his, then dusted her hands and placed them on her hips. Which had the unfortunate effect of drawing his attention to the hourglass waist hidden inside her simple gray dress.

Desire heated his blood.

"You know you're only making it more impossible for me to let you go." He smiled.

She flashed back a defiant grin. Then it faded. "I can't stay."

Her pulse fluttered at her neck and he resisted a sudden, fierce urge to press his lips to the quivering, warm skin.

"I'm afraid I can't let you go."

She let out a sharp laugh. "You can't *let* me? Off with her head? Those days are over, even if you are a prince."

He laughed. "A beheading does sound counterproductive. But I do insist you give the ancient, sovereign nation of Caspia at least the customary two weeks' notice." A plan blossomed in his mind. "You must come to Caspia with me. Immediately."

"Oh."

A tiny fire lit inside her eyes. Good.

"I need you to arrange an immediate meeting of the principals of Caspia Designs. The chief executives of each of the subsidiary brands *must* be there, no matter what it takes to bring them."

He watched for her reaction. The prospect of cajoling pleasure-seeking European plutocrats into attending to actual business might make some people quit on the spot.

But not Tessa. A glow of appreciation filled him as she simply nodded.

"To be honest, when I took the job, I hoped it would involve some travel. I'd be glad to come to Caspia before I go."

Had he truly never taken her to Caspia before? Surely he'd remember the vision of all that golden hair being tossed by the sea breeze. He'd grown to think of travel as a tiresome necessity. He clapped his hands together. "We'll fly tomorrow in my private plane. Arrange for a 2:00 p.m. departure."

Energy surged through him as his plan took shape. This trip would take Tessa's mind off that divorce-mongering cad who wanted to steal her away from him.

Not that his interest in her was personal, of course. He took both business and pleasure very seriously, which meant keeping them strictly separate.

But the charms of Caspia—combined with some judicious charm on his part—would soon make Tessa realize she'd been crazy to ever think of leaving.

Two

Relief surged through Sebastian as he grasped his old friend's hand in a warm handshake. Reed Wellington was the kind of man you wanted on your side in a crisis. His clear blue eyes never reflected a hint of worry.

"Sebastian, I'm sorry I couldn't make the snowboarding trip to Kilimanjaro, but Elizabeth thought it sounded, well, crazy."

Sebastian laughed. "I guess that's the problem with being married. You wind up stuck with someone who truly cares about you."

"Yes. And you have to stop hurling yourself off mountaintops." His eyes crinkled into a smile. "When are you going to get married, eh?"

"Never. Or when I meet the right woman. Whichever comes first." He got this question a lot.

"No one can accuse you of not trying your best to bed every eligible woman in the world."

"Just doing my royal duty."

"Seriously, isn't there a lot of pressure on you to sire the next heir to the throne of Caspia?"

"I try not to think about that. Besides, we Caspians often live to be over a hundred and my father's barely sixty."

"All that goats' milk yogurt, huh?"

"Food of the gods."

They shared a chuckle but Sebastian couldn't help thinking Reed's laugh was a little too hearty. Forced, even. And what was it with married people trying to shove eternal bondage down your throat?

"You're here about Caspia Designs?" Reed gestured for him to sit in the leather chair opposite the wide walnut desk. The room was decorated like the headquarters of an eighteenth-century shipping magnate.

Sebastian eased himself into the chair. "I am. I'm in dire need of your business expertise. I'm afraid the company is in worse financial shape than I'd suspected."

Reed's expression changed to one of concern. "How so?"

"Until I took over the reins a year ago, Caspia Designs was overseen by Deon Maridis, an old and close friend of my father's. He's a good man, but the company's profits went into a slow slide under his watch."

Sebastian fought an urge to loosen his collar. "Last year the company actually lost money."

"What?" Reed sat up. "I confess luxury brands are not my area of expertise, and I can imagine the company is mature and not growing much, but Caspia Designs owns some of the most renowned luxury brands in the world. Aria cars, Bugaretti Jewels, LeVerge Champagne, Carriage

Leathers…Why, I bought my wife one of their bags last Christmas and it nearly bankrupted me." He laughed for a second, then frowned. "How can they be losing money?"

Sebastian leaned forward. "Our brands have been known as the best of the best since the 1920s when the company went public, but many of them have barely changed since. Production methods are outdated and inefficient, and there's been little effort to attract new customers. There are now a host of luxury jewelers, vintners and the like, and most of them have better distribution and marketing than the ones owned by Caspia Designs. I want to shake up the companies and get them operating like a real business. I also plan to market the goods to a younger audience."

"Sounds as if you need to do some rebranding. Like Burberry and Mini Cooper."

"Exactly."

Reed tilted his head and smiled. "Sort of like you've been doing with Caspia."

Sebastian couldn't help a swell of pride. "It's true. Ten years ago, Caspia had virtually no foreign investors, no tourism, little business beyond those that had existed for hundreds of years."

Reed raised an eyebrow. "Now you have hotels and luxury boutiques and restaurants for tourists to spend their money in. And you accomplished it almost single-handedly over the last ten years."

"My assistant, Tessa, must get some of the credit." Her green eyes flashed in his mind. "She's an organizational genius."

"You're lucky to have her."

"Don't I know it." Sebastian's fist clenched. How could

she plan to abandon him at a time like this? "And we'll be working hard to make Caspia Designs a good investment for all our shareholders."

"I don't doubt you'll succeed."

"I intend to, but I'm used to building from scratch, not fixing something that's broken. I need your advice on how to turn the individual companies around, and fast."

"Hmm." Reed tapped his gold pen on his blotter. "If I were you, I'd start by scheduling a meeting with the President and CEO—or their equivalents—of each company within Caspia Designs. Get them all together and read them the riot act."

"I've already asked Tessa to schedule a meeting."

"Excellent. At that meeting, challenge them to come up with ten ways to immediately increase market share and profitability in their own company." He gave Sebastian a series of examples of companies who'd effected a similar change by bringing in experienced managers or reinventing their product for modern markets. "You could hire a consulting firm to investigate and give you additional ideas."

"I prefer to solve our problems internally. These are all businesses with quality products. They've been resting on their laurels, and it's time to shake them up."

"I can see them shaking already. You can do anything you set your mind to. Even snowboarding down Kilimanjaro." He leaned back with a wistful smile.

Sebastian's chest filled with regret that his friend had missed the experience. "You should have been there."

Reed looked away, picked up a pen and tapped it on his blotter. "Yes. Well. I have other commitments now." A muscle twitched at his temple. His blue gaze seemed less bright than usual.

"How is Elizabeth? I haven't seen her in a long time. Is she still your secret weapon on the doubles court, as well as the love of your life?"

Reed's eyes crinkled. "She sure is. We'll have to get together for a game sometime with you and whoever your current mixed-doubles partner is."

Sebastian shrugged. "I'm playing singles at the moment. Got business to take care of."

"Even if we don't see you on the courts, you must come to our anniversary party."

"What is it, three years?"

"Five." Reed's jaw stiffened.

Not the most reassuring indication of marital bliss.

"That's great." He leaned over the desk and slapped Reed on the arm. Tried to sound enthusiastic. "Just let me know where to show up. And you know the two of you have an open invitation to visit Caspia again whenever you like."

"I'll take you up on that soon. Right now I'm in the throes of starting a new company. It's sucking up even more of my free time than all that partying we used to do when we were younger."

"Who says I've stopped?" Sebastian raised a brow.

"You always did have impressive stamina. One day you'll meet a woman you actually want to stay home with."

"So they tell me, but I don't plan to wave the white flag of surrender anytime soon."

The doorman pulled open the door and Sebastian stepped into the lobby of his building. Vivian Vannick-Smythe's two fluffy white dogs stopped scratching at the priceless Oriental rug and turned to growl at him.

If that woman led him around on a string all day, he wouldn't be in a good mood, either. Sebastian shot the dogs a sympathetic glance.

"Prince Sebastian!" Vivian turned to him with a winning smile. Or had too much plastic surgery left her expression permanently fixed like that?

"Hello, Vivian."

"How lovely to see you here. I noticed you haven't been around much lately."

"I've been in Caspia."

"Ahh." Her dogs lunged at his pant leg, yowling and snapping at the end of their embroidered leashes. "I read about those nasty storms in the Mediterranean. I do hope Caspia didn't suffer too much damage."

"There were some losses to the olive crops, but happily no one was hurt."

"What a relief. Backward countries do seem to suffer the most from these things."

Sebastian's hackles shot up. "Caspia is in no way backward. If you were to visit…" *Perish the thought.* "You'd find a thriving, modern country on the brink of becoming one of the prime luxury tourist destinations in the world."

"How charmingly passionate you are about your homeland."

Sebastian glanced up to see if the elevator was coming. *Yes, thank God.*

The doors opened and Vivian's paisley skirt swirled about her ankles as she walked in. Her dogs yapped around Sebastian's ankles, loud in the enclosed space.

"Hold the elevator!" A deep voice rang across the marbled lobby.

Sebastian looked up to see Gage Lattimer diving past the doorman.

Vivian's dogs diverted their hostile intentions to him. Fortunately for Sebastian, Vivian followed suit.

"Why, Gage, our man of mystery. I was just chatting with Prince Sebastian." She shone that fixed smile on him. "He should be a role model to you. He does live up to his clean-cut image."

Clean-cut? Sebastian resisted the urge to test his chin for stubble. He'd been called a lot of things, but clean-cut wasn't one of them. Maybe she meant the suit?

He shot a puzzled look at Gage.

"Are you implying something?" Gage raised an eyebrow at Vivian.

"Moi?" She forced a laugh. "Of course not. I believe people's personal affairs should be kept private."

Gage shook his head.

An awkward silence thickened in the air. Well, not exactly silence, what with all the growling.

Sebastian's muscles unwound a bit when the elevator reached his floor. He held the door open for Vivian to exit, her leashed demons scampering ahead of her.

Unfortunately they lived on the same floor.

Happily the walls were thick.

Her dogs wiggled with excitement as she fumbled in her purse for her key. They actually looked sort of adorable for once and he couldn't resist crouching to pet one of the fluffy fur balls.

It turned and snapped at him, almost catching his finger.

Never mind.

Sebastian's apartment had a neglected air. His former house sitter, Carrie Gray, hadn't left his employ to marry that long ago, but already stacks of unopened mail tilted precariously on the hall table. He picked an envelope off the top and ripped it open.

"You are cordially invited to celebrate the landmark status of our building."

He snorted.

Yes, 721 Park Avenue was a beautiful building, but it probably wasn't much over a hundred years old. Parts of the royal palace in Caspia were rumored to be five thousand years old.

That was a landmark.

He flung the envelope back on the pile and lifted his foot to step over the bag he'd dropped in the foyer the night before. He'd gone straight from the plane to the office to an all-night party and hadn't had time to unpack. It was inconvenient having no one to do it for him.

But the bag wasn't there.

Did he hear voices?

He did. Female voices.

Interesting. Especially since he hadn't brought anyone home last night.

Anticipation pricked through him as he walked down the marble-floored hallway toward the living room.

A familiar mane of blond hair cascaded over the back of an uncomfortable eighteenth-century chair. "Tessa."

She jumped. "Oh, Your Highness, I didn't hear you come in."

"Your Highness?" He lifted a brow.

"I'm interviewing candidates for your new house sitter." She indicated a red-haired girl seated opposite her.

He smiled at them both. He always could count on Tessa to handle everything.

* * *

Tessa excused herself for a moment and hurried after Sebastian. "I unpacked your bag. I'm not sure if I did it right. Let me show you where I put things."

She rambled on, suddenly feeling like an intruder in his private space. His house sitter used to handle the apartment, so she rarely came here. She was embarrassed that she still hadn't had time to tackle his mail. "I didn't mean to surprise you. I just thought it would be a good idea to interview the house sitters here so they'd have an idea of what the job entails. The antiques and all. You can tell a lot about someone by the way they treat your home."

"Good thinking."

She rushed along the hallway. Why was she so anxious? Perhaps because she was also secretly interviewing for her own replacement.

"The agency had three girls ready this morning, and I didn't want to wait, or to interrupt you at Reed's. How did the meeting go?"

"Great. I wanted to get his advice on how to bring Caspia Designs into the twenty-first century." He glanced at her. "Or even the twentieth."

His mischievous grin made her heart beat faster.

"You'll turn the company around fast."

"With your help." He shot her a dark look. "Starting with this trip to Caspia."

She swallowed. Even poring over the inadequate and whimsical financial reports of Caspia Designs had made her fall a little bit in love with the country. It seemed a land ruled by passion rather than politics. Exuberance rather than economics.

Much like its devastatingly handsome prince.

Tessa bit her lip. Already she'd reconsidered her plan to leave. Sebastian paid her well and treated her kindly. Her parents told her she was mad to quit a job with such excellent benefits.

But she'd spent most of her adult life working with the rich and famous, first at a PR firm and now here. She was sick of glitz and glamour. She'd trade it in a heartbeat for the simple happiness her parents still shared after nearly fifty years of marriage.

For some reason being tall and blond attracted the biggest jerk in every room she entered. She'd had enough of being arm-candy for movers and shakers who weren't interested in anything beyond a night of sex.

Normal "regular guy" types *never* asked her out. Patrick was the best thing to happen to her in a long time. Yes, he was a high-profile lawyer, but he was down-to-earth and practical. He called when he said he would. He took her out on dates—when he had the time—and treated her with respect.

Something she'd begun to worry would never happen.

In his large, uncluttered bedroom, Sebastian removed his jacket and started to unbutton his shirt. Tessa dragged her eyes away. "I hung your pants and shirts in the closet. And I put your…underwear in the drawer."

Her cheeks heated. Handling his boxers had felt way too personal.

"You didn't have to do that." His fingers continued down his buttons. He tugged his shirt out of his pants to undo the bottom ones and she fought an urge to run for the door.

But she didn't want him to know that watching him undress affected her. He was probably used to undressing in front of…staff. It meant nothing to him.

She meant nothing to him.

For years she'd been telling herself her silly attraction to her boss would fade over time. She'd fall for someone else.

But other men seemed pale and uninteresting compared to Sebastian.

Except Patrick, of course. He was thoughtful. Nice. Considerate.

He wasn't quite ready for fatherhood yet, but maybe once his big case was over and they settled into a comfortable house in a nice quiet neighborhood with trees and grass and…

Uh-oh. Sebastian's long fingers undid the button on his pants.

She headed for the door. "I put your toiletries in the bathroom. Well, your toothbrush. I didn't see anything else."

"I don't need anything else."

"I'll get back to my interview." Her voice was high and squeaky. She heard the swish of his pants sliding over his long, muscled legs.

"Did Dior Homme send the T-shirts?"

"Um. Yes. I put them…" She'd have to go back into the bedroom to find the shelf. Squinting to avoid the vision of a seminaked Sebastian, she hurried to the closet.

"Here, on the middle shelf." The fresh pile of shirts commemorated the deal he'd brokered to open a Dior boutique in the row of luxury stores along the harbor in Caspia. She picked up a large black T-shirt with a geometric design and held it toward him while keeping her eyes averted.

She could smell his scent. Soap and skin. A hint of sweat.

How could that get her blood pumping? He was just a *guy,* for crying out loud. Patrick smelled much nicer, of that woodsy cologne he wore. Which, actually, she hated. But she could buy him another.

"Tessa."

She turned without thinking. At the exact moment he lifted the T-shirt over his head and flexed all the muscles of his wide, bronzed chest.

Her knees buckled and she struggled to stay upright.

Not a problem. She didn't like big muscles anyway. Too brutish.

She preferred men who were…cerebral.

"What do you think?" He indicated the T-shirt freshly pulled over his thick pecs.

"Nice design." Her voice came out weird and flat. A light dusting of black hair roughened his hard, bare thighs below the T-shirt hem.

"Yeah. I like this new line. Did you take some for yourself?"

"I don't wear extra large."

"You could wear them in bed." His low voice tickled her ears.

Tessa's eyes widened. Her face heated. Sebastian was thinking about her in bed?

Oh. Get over yourself.

If anyone knew that women like to sleep in oversize T-shirts, it was Sebastian. He'd seen a lot of women in bed.

"Sure. I'll grab a couple."

"Great." He shot her a white-toothed smile.

That set her on alert. Why was he smiling at her for no reason?

*Because he wants to keep you around as his serf, orga-
nizing his files and answering his phone, dummy.*

"I'll go finish the interview."

"I appreciate it. I'm going out to grab something to eat.
You want anything from the café?"

"I'm fine. Thanks for asking."

Again, the niceness. Very suspicious.

Sebastian strode across the room, legs still bare. He slid
a hand under his T-shirt to scratch his rock-hard belly
while he contemplated his impressive collection of jeans.

Tessa managed to rasp, "See you later," as she rushed
out the door.

The Park Café was the closest eatery, so Sebastian went
there often when he was in town. He'd spent several weeks
in New York in the spring and had hand-trained one of the
young servers to make the perfect cup of coffee—or at
least the closest possible approximation available in this
part of the world.

His heart sank as he entered the bright space of the
café to a sea of new faces. Then he spotted Reed and
Elizabeth Wellington sitting at one of the café tables. He
waved and tried to catch their eye, but they were deep in
conversation.

"What can I get you?" asked the perky young server.

"I'd like a pastrami on rye with Russian dressing and
nothing else. And a seven-shot espresso."

She vanished, her expressionless face imparting confidence. What a relief not to be peppered with questions
about lettuce and tomatoes and mayo.

His synapses tingled in anticipation of a welcome jolt
of caffeine.

He glanced over at his friends' table. Reed leaned forward, talking in hushed tones, while his wife looked strangely tight-lipped. Were they arguing?

The server returned with seven tiny china cups of espresso. *Here we go again.* "In one cup, please."

She picked up a paper cup and began to pour them in.

"They'll be too cool. Could you use china and heat it again?" He kept his voice pleasant.

"Milk and sugar?"

"No milk, no sugar, no cinnamon, no froth, no chocolate curls. Just the coffee."

His sandwich appeared, loaded with unwanted vegetables.

Sebastian rubbed a hand over his face.

He'd be home in Caspia soon.

"I don't think you do!" A raised voice caught his attention and he turned to see Reed, who'd stood suddenly, scraping his chair back on the tile floor.

Elizabeth looked panic-stricken. "Please, Reed…" he heard her say, before the server plunked his big mug of espresso on the counter.

He swiped his credit card and turned in time to see Reed striding out of the restaurant, a black expression clouding his chiseled features.

Alarmed, Sebastian glanced at Elizabeth, who stared after her husband with a stunned look on her face.

Sebastian snatched his cup and plate off the counter and hurried to the table. He sat without waiting for an invitation.

His gut twisted when he saw her eyes brimming with unshed tears. "Elizabeth, what's wrong?"

He reached for her hand but she snatched it up and

dabbed at her eyes with the napkin. "Nothing! Nothing at all. I'm fine." A sob belied her words. "Allergies. They're terrible at this time of year." She drew in a sharp breath. "How are you, Sebastian?"

"Once I've had this coffee, I'll be okay." He took a bracing sip. Elizabeth was obviously in distress and it pained him not to be able to help her. "Can I get you something? Some chocolate?"

She laughed. "Chocolate usually does help, doesn't it?" She glanced toward the door. "But not today. I have to run, I have an appointment." Hands shaking, she gathered her handbag and a large shopping bag. "I'm sorry I don't have more time to chat. I've—" Her voice caught.

Something was very wrong.

"I understand. Another time." The platitudes felt hollow and useless, but she clearly didn't want to talk.

He rose from his chair and kissed her cheek. Cold as ice. "And, Elizabeth, if you ever need anything, anything at all, don't hesitate to call me."

She nodded and hurried away.

How odd. She and Reed always seemed like the perfect couple. Their wedding had been the social event of the season, the bride radiant, her handsome groom the toast of the city for months. Sebastian had even found himself contemplating the joys of marriage—for a week or two.

Luckily it had worn off.

Five years later and here they were: arguments, tension, tears.

Marriage did not look like fun.

Three

Sebastian brimmed with anticipation as he marched across the tarmac toward the plane. "Tessa!"

At the sound of his voice, she looked up and smiled. "Hello, Sebastian."

She stood at the bottom of the movable stairs, fiddling with the strap on her bag. The wind molded her thin dress to her body in a way that made his blood pressure jump a notch.

Her legs were endless. Slender and shapely. The kind of legs that could wrap around you and hold you in a vise of pleasure.

Not that he had any intention of seducing his assistant into bed.

Even he had his limits.

At least he thought he did.

"Don't be nervous. Our pilot is very experienced. Have you met Sven?"

"Yes, he introduced himself. I'm more excited than nervous. I actually love to fly. It's fun seeing the world from above."

"I do agree." A smile settled over his face as he took her elbow and led her up the stairs.

Sebastian refused to discuss work during the flight. He wanted Tessa to relax and enjoy herself. To banish any thoughts that she was bored and ready to "move on."

Any "moving on" would be accomplished in his comfortably appointed jet. "Champagne?" He lifted a bottle out of the fridge.

Tessa's eyes widened. "It's only two o'clock."

"That means it's eight in Caspia. They always say to pack and dress for your destination, so why not drink for it, too?"

He popped the cork.

Tessa bit her lip. "Okay. You're the boss."

"Exactly. You'd better do as I say." He handed her the glass. "Here's to your maiden voyage to Caspia." He clinked his glass against hers.

Excitement sparkled in her big, green eyes. "I've never left the country before."

"You're kidding?"

"Nope. I flew around a bit on business for my first job, but mostly to L.A. I've never been to Europe."

"Not even to visit friends?" Sebastian found this hard to believe. He knew quite a few people who went to boarding school with Tessa and they were as likely to be found on the ski slopes of Gstaad or the beaches of Provence as in their Wall Street watering holes.

Tessa put her champagne glass on the table. "I went to St. Peter's on a scholarship." She raised her eyes to meet his at the mention of the highbrow prep school. "I'm not really one of them."

"One of who?"

"You know, the jet set, or whatever you want to call it."

She looked so anxious that he managed to suppress the smile tugging at his lips. "Um, Tessa, I hate to be the one to break this to you, but you're sitting in a jet right now, waiting to take off."

She swatted his idea away with a movement of her graceful hands. "You know what I mean. This is part of my job."

Sebastian slammed his glass down next to hers. "I don't want to hear anything more about any *job*. You are vital to the economic growth of the nation of Caspia. You have a *career* with us."

He'd make it a personal challenge to make sure she stayed. He did enjoy a challenge. The curse of a competitive nature.

"Buckle up." Sven's voice came over the radio. Sebastian watched as Tessa fastened her buckle over her slim hips. Her long fingers were magnificent. He could imagine them dancing over the strings of a Caspian harp.

Or over the muscles of his belly. And lower. Between his thighs...

He shifted in his seat. "Sven, let's take the temperature down a couple of degrees."

Tessa looked sideways at him. "Do we have to hold on to our glasses?"

"Can't hurt." Sebastian swept hers up and handed it to her. Their fingers brushed for an electric moment. He sipped the dry Blanc de Noirs, but the sparkle of the bubbles only increased an intriguing sense of anticipation that crackled through him.

Tessa peered out the window as the plane lifted over the ocean, her long neck craned forward. "Goodness, New York really is a bunch of islands, isn't it? Wow, what a beach. The breakers look awesome from up here. And I can see a fishing boat! I never think of people fishing near the city. And look at all those swimming pools on Long Island. Don't these people know there's an ocean right there?"

Her eyes shone, dazzled with sights he'd long ceased to notice.

Sebastian laughed.

Caspia with Tessa was going to be fun.

Tessa couldn't help feeling a little sad as their plane approached their final destination in the dead of night.

All across Europe, towns and cities had glittered amongst vast swathes of dark countryside. Snowcapped mountain ranges shimmered in the faint glow of the moon.

That same moon reflected off calm ocean water as the plane banked on approach to the airport in Caspia. Giddy from champagne and from chatting with Sebastian about everything under the sun, she couldn't imagine getting any sleep before morning.

The plane landed on the runway with barely a bump. Sebastian peered out the window. "My driver is waiting. We'll be at the palace in ten minutes."

The palace.

Tessa's skin grew tight as terror crept over her.

An actual palace with a real king and queen living in it.

She glanced sideways at Sebastian. He was stretching, which had the unfortunate effect of pulling his black T-shirt tight over the granite-hard expanse of his chest.

She jerked her eyes away. In addition to being a royal prince, he was her boss, for crying out loud.

Her heart hammered as the pilot opened the door and ushered them down the steps. Sebastian gestured for her to go first, so she stepped out into the dark night.

A cool breeze rushed her face, rich with the smell of the sea.

"Home sweet home." Sebastian drew in a hearty lungful. "I find it harder and harder to leave and each time I return, I'm more grateful than ever."

"I guess that's good, since you couldn't really leave anyway, could you?" How odd to grow up with the obligation of being a monarch some day. To have no choice in who or what you could become.

"No one truly leaves Caspia. Even when you depart, you'll always carry a piece of her with you."

His voice echoed with such gravitas that she glanced back to see if he was joking.

Apparently not.

He stared straight ahead, his strong features highlighted in the airport floodlights. "Dmitri!" He waved at the uniformed chauffeur standing in front of a long, black limousine. "I'd like you to meet Tessa, my right-hand woman."

Dmitri nodded. Sebastian's odd introduction gave her a little surge of pride. She wouldn't mind being the right hand on so sturdy and capable a body.

The limo drove them swiftly to the palace, where people materialized out of the darkness to carry their bags.

A lamp-lit passage led to a cool atrium with a trickling fountain. Two young men rushed forward to ply them with damp towels and glasses of cool water.

Flustered, Tessa watched Sebastian as he wiped his face vigorously with the towel. She didn't want to smear the plush, white cotton with her makeup so she used it to pat her neck.

The water had a deliciously sweet taste, and she finished the whole glass in one draft. As soon as she was done, a man with a jug refilled it.

"Thanks," she murmured, before sipping again.

So this is what it was like to be waited on hand and foot. Kind of weird, but she could see how you'd get used to it. She tried hard not to giggle.

Just nerves.

"I'll walk Tessa to her room," Sebastian declared. Her skin tingled as he slipped his warm, strong arm inside hers in a proprietary gesture that made her blush.

It was all so strange. Mosaics glittered under her feet. Stone pillars flanked the wide hallway. They walked through the silent palace, the darkness of night softened only by light from wall sconces.

At the end of another long hallway, Sebastian led her through an open pair of double doors into the most glorious room she'd ever seen.

A vast bed filled the center of the huge chamber. Silk curtains billowed from a central point in the ceiling and cascaded down to form a luxurious canopy. The bed itself was lush with patterned pillows and soft-looking covers.

If there were a pea under that mattress, it wouldn't bother her one bit.

"I hope you'll be comfortable. You can ring this bell if you need anything." He pointed to a tiny golden bell, resting on a magnificent gold-inlaid dressing table. "Or call me on my cell." He yawned. "I need some shut-eye."

He closed the door behind him as he left.

In a panic, Tessa realized she didn't have her bag. She rushed to the door, then the open closet caught her eye.

Her clothes hung inside it.

She inhaled, and walked over. Yes, they were really her clothes, with her unpacked duffel bag placed neatly on the floor of the closet.

She swallowed and lifted her nightgown from a hanger. She'd splurged on a gauzy white cotton gown, trimmed with lace, that seemed appropriate for sleeping in a palace.

In front of the magnificent silk-draped bed, however, her nightgown looked more suitable for a milkmaid.

She changed, washed her face at the polished brass basin in the bathroom and brushed out her hair.

She stood for a moment at one of the long windows, holding the heavy drape back. Pale moonlight poured onto the floor at her feet, making the mosaic sparkle.

She climbed onto the cloudlike softness of the high bed, under the layered canopy.

She really should call Patrick in New York. She'd promised to let him know she arrived safely. He'd insisted on knowing every detail of her itinerary so he could get in touch with her at any time.

He was just like that. Caring.

But surely he wouldn't mind if she called first thing in the morning?

It was nearly nine when Tessa finally awoke and peered at her watch in the curtained gloom. She could hear noise outside the windows, the distant honking of car horns, the mutter of conversations, even a clatter of hooves.

She sprang off the bed and hurried to the window. Bright golden sunshine streamed in as she parted the curtains.

Wow.

The room had a magnificent view over the city. White-washed buildings clung to the hillsides, their simple, organic shapes suggesting that they'd been there almost as long as the land itself.

The procession of crisp, white walls descended gradually toward a wide bay. Long seawalls created from massive stone blocks encompassed the harbor like two welcoming arms, the sea within them as calm as a pond.

The whole effect was like something out of an ancient myth. She half expected to see Helen of Troy sail into the harbor on a trireme rowed by a hundred oarsmen.

But modern life intruded cheerfully on the ancient splendor. Cars wound up and down the hill toward the harbor. Laughter and the strains of a Madonna hit mingled with the song of birds that fluttered back and forth between tall cypress trees.

Her cell chimed and vibrated on the dresser. She rushed to grab it. Patrick.

"Hi."

"I've been worried sick. I even checked the airline flight data to see if there were reports of an accident. Why didn't you call?"

"Oh, we got here so late and I was tired. It's sweet of you to worry, but really, I'm fine."

"Do you have your own room?"

She laughed. "No, I'm in the harem with all the king's wives." He didn't laugh back. "Of course I have my own room, silly. And it's so beautiful. But I'm not sure my blow-dryer will work here."

"Do be careful of the voltage. You never know what to expect with foreign wiring. I am worried about you being all alone in a foreign country."

"I'm not alone. I'm with Sebastian."

"I know."

When she finally got Patrick off the phone with assurances that she had not been killed in a midair collision or sold into slavery, she had a quick shower. As she suspected, her dryer was a useless lump of plastic and metal since the wall outlet was a different shape than her plug. She towel dried her hair as best she could and was putting moisturizer on her face when she heard a knock on the door.

She almost dropped the bottle. "Come in?" The uncertainty in her own voice made her even more nervous.

The door flung open. Sebastian stood silhouetted against the bright corridor. "I trust you slept well."

His soft voice wrapped around her like the warm morning breeze.

"I did." She pushed back a hank of her still-damp hair. "I can't get over how lovely it is here."

He smiled. "You've seen nothing yet. Come, eat." He held out his arm for her to take it. He wore a collarless white linen shirt. Tailored black pants added to the impression of casual elegance.

Not that she cared what her boss wore.

Tessa walked across the room, the skirt of her pale green dress swishing around her legs, then matched his long stride down the colonnaded hallway.

He directed her into another wide, bright chamber. Floor-to-ceiling frescoes depicted a magnificent procession of men and horses, pennants flying.

Tessa tugged her gaze from the art and focused on the other people in the room. A middle-aged man and woman sat at one end of a long, white stone table.

"Mama, this is Tessa, my New York assistant."

The woman rose from her carved chair, tall and graceful, her silver hair pulled back into a chignon. She held out a heavily ringed hand and Tessa hurried forward to shake it.

"It's an honor," murmured Tessa, attempting a curtsey. This was *The Queen*.

"And this is my dad."

Tessa shook his offered hand. "It's a pleasure to meet you, Your Majesty."

Maybe he heard her voice shake, but the king patted her hand gently and looked at her with the kindest eyes she'd ever seen. "The pleasure is all mine, my dear."

He also had silver hair, with patches of black above his ears that indicated it must once have been as dark as Sebastian's.

"What'd the cook rustle up for us this morning?" Sebastian reached forward and grabbed a rasher of bacon, then popped it in his mouth. "Mmm." He pulled out a chair for Tessa, directly opposite the queen. She slid into it as gracefully as she could.

A plate materialized in front of her immediately, borne by a silent servant.

"Do help yourself, dear," the queen said in perfect, British-accented English. "If you don't see anything you like, we can have something prepared."

"Oh, that won't be necessary, it all looks marvelous."

Tessa had no appetite whatsoever in the presence of three crowned heads—including Sebastian. She'd never paid much attention to his being a prince before, perhaps because the whole concept of royalty seemed rather alien back in the States. Amidst the splendor of the royal palace, however, it was impossible to forget.

Sebastian offered her various dishes, and she took a small amount of each. Eggs scrambled with herbs, freshly baked rolls covered in fragrant sesame seeds, crispy bacon and spicy sausages, fresh peaches and plums, sliced and laid in an interwoven pattern, and a dish of creamy yogurt with sweet, golden honey.

"Tessa, what part of the States are you from?" The queen's question had a tone of mild interrogation.

"Connecticut."

"A lovely state. Are you near Greenwich?"

"Yes, very close." In geography. In lifestyle, though, a million miles.

Tessa hated saying where she was from. Wealthy and privileged people immediately assumed she was one of them. It was embarrassing for everyone when they eventually found out she wasn't.

That's when she learned who her real friends were.

She had to give Sebastian credit. He hadn't blinked when she told him she was a scholarship student.

But why would he care? She was just his employee.

"And what does your father do, dear?" The queen lifted an elegantly arched brow.

Jeez. Was she back in high school? Rich people could be very predictable. "He's retired now."

She sipped her juice. Partly to prevent her tongue from saying, *He's a retired school custodian. Yes, you heard right, he cleaned the school. Not quite what you were expecting, was it?*

The queen's tight smile did nothing to soothe her churning stomach. Suddenly she wished she was back home, under the covers in her familiar apartment.

Still, she attempted to act normal and make polite conversation during the meal, instead of gazing around the room and gawking at her companions.

It wasn't easy.

When the king and queen left the room together, it was all she could do not to sag in her chair in relief.

"More yogurt?" Sebastian lifted the ornate golden urn that looked as though it had been passed down at least ten generations.

"No, thanks. I really should get to work. Would you please show me where the files are? I want to dig out what we'll need for the meeting."

"Absolutely not." He rose in a swift motion. "We have far more important things to do."

"Like what?"

"You must see our country. More coffee?"

"No, thanks, I'm fine. I might blast off if I drink more of that stuff."

"Good, right?"

She couldn't resist smiling in response to his enthusiastic grin. "Fantastic." Her toes tingled at the idea of exploring the world she'd glimpsed from her window. "Could we go see the harbor?"

"Of course." Sebastian rose from his chair and held out his hand for her to take it.

He never did that at the office.

Tessa slid her fingers into his strong hand, and let him pull her from her chair. He didn't move out of the way as she stood, so she found herself dangerously close to his muscled chest. His warm, male scent of sunshine and spice.

Her skin prickled at his nearness.

Why didn't he move?

His dark eyes drifted over her pale green dress. "You look lovely today, Tessa."

"Thanks." She swallowed.

He never usually noticed what she was wearing.

He hadn't let go of her hand, either. Her palm heated against his.

What was he up to?

Four

"**Y**our hair is wavy." Sebastian's gaze followed the undulating mass of hair that she'd tied back with a clasp before breakfast.

Tessa's hand sprang self-consciously to her head. At least it was nearly dry. "My dryer didn't fit the outlet."

Sebastian reached behind her head, his arm almost brushing her cheek in a swift movement that made her gasp. With thumb and finger he unsnapped her hair clip and removed it. Her hair tumbled down her back.

His eyes shone with appreciation. "You should always wear it like this." He pocketed her clip. "Why do women scorch the natural beauty out of their hair?"

"It looks neater blow-dried straight."

"I disagree." He reached into her hair.

Tessa fought the urge to protest. This was totally unprofessional! He stroked her hair. Heat rippled in her belly and she swallowed the desire to purr like a contented cat.

She gulped for air. Had he forgotten she had a boyfriend? "Where are we heading?"

"The harbor. I'll phone ahead and have my boat prepared."

He withdrew his hand from her hair and reached into his pocket for his cell.

Oh, how the other half lived.

Tessa expected a chauffeured limousine—especially since that's how Sebastian generally moved around New York.

But no. They left the palace on foot, through an arched doorway that took them out onto one of the winding cobbled streets flanked with whitewashed buildings.

She was even more astonished when Sebastian stopped to greet ordinary citizens. He seemed to know everyone on a first-name basis, and inquired after their families and their businesses like an old friend.

Weirder still, Tessa found she could understand snatches of conversation, although she'd never had the need to learn the Caspian language.

After a few introductions, she made a halting attempt to greet an elderly man in Caspian.

Sebastian rewarded her efforts with a broad grin. "You speak like a native."

"No, I don't! But I'm having fun trying. How come so many of the words sound familiar?"

"Did you study Latin in school?"

"I went to St. Peter's." She chuckled. "You know the snootiest prep school on the East Coast made everyone take Latin."

"That's why you understand us. Caspians speak a dialect of Latin that's changed little since the time of the

Roman Empire. Add a vowel at the end of a few words, and you're speaking Caspian. Some words haven't changed at all. *Te amo,* for example, still means *I love you.*"

Mischief sparkled in his eyes.

Tessa ignored the rush of heat to her chest. He was toying with her! What a nerve. Just because she'd handed in her notice he thought he could let loose and flirt with her before she quit?

Te amo. Yeah. Right. As if she was dumb enough to join the cohorts of women notched on his bedpost. Maybe he thought it would be fun to make her fall in love with him—then dump her—as punishment for quitting her job and leaving him in the lurch.

Sebastian had a reputation for treating seduction as a sport. His little black book—little BlackBerry, rather—must have a thousand names in it. She knew about all those starlets and models and fashion designers, not to mention tennis star Andrea Raditz and soccer champion Leah Mannion. Oh, yes, and half his graduating class at Brown University. And let's not even get into all those British girls he'd romanced during his years at Eton.

Loving Sebastian was a game with a very crowded playing field, and she had no intention of joining in.

When they reached the end of a row of stuccoed buildings, Tessa stood facing the magnificent bay she'd seen from her room.

The sea breeze cooled her, and the salt air mingled with the sharp scent of lemons piled high on a nearby market stall.

"This scene looks as if it hasn't changed in two thousand years."

"It probably hasn't, at least on the surface. The wireless

Internet is pretty recent." He flashed a sly smile. "No one's sure who first built this harbor. It's been here for all of recorded history."

They walked toward the water. Almost turquoise in the shallow bay, it lapped against ancient blocks of stone worn smooth by the passage of a million feet.

A long painted boat bobbed a few feet offshore, and Sebastian waved to the man seated in its prow. He punted the boat alongside the quay, and lashed it to a giant iron ring.

The boatman was young and handsome. Tessa found herself held on both sides by gorgeous Caspian men as she stepped down into the rocking, red interior.

Sebastian jumped in after her. He landed so lightly on his feet, the boat barely twitched. "Feels good to be back on the water. A true Caspian gets edgy on dry land for too long."

He settled back into a red velvet banquette that spanned the width of the boat. "Give us the full tour, Dino. Tessa has never been to our country before."

"That is deprivation, indeed," said Dino, in unaccented English.

"Ita vero," agreed Tessa in Latin.

Sebastian grinned. "Show-off."

Tessa raised an eyebrow. "Yeah, and?"

He leaned back on the seat and once again wove his long fingers into the thick, loose mass of her untamed hair. "I like a woman who's not afraid to show what she's made of," he whispered.

Dino tactfully kept his eyes on the harbor wall as they rowed toward it.

Tessa's blood heated with a mix of excitement and

confusion. Her nipples rose to meet the delicate chiffon of her summery dress, and she became instantly aware that they were likely visible, since the strappy design didn't allow for a bra.

"What impressive stonework," she exclaimed, to draw Sebastian's eyes away. The last thing she needed was for him to think she was aroused. "How did they get it here?"

"Historians speculate that they floated the huge carved blocks out there on wooden rafts. They also talk about a giant golden statue that used to guard the entrance to the harbor."

"What happened to it?"

"Some people think it's buried under the sand out there. A team of archaeologists once tried to find it, but they couldn't. With new sonar technologies, though, it might be worth another look."

"Could be an interesting tourist attraction."

"Exactly."

Attracting people to Caspia was a passion of Sebastian's. Now that she was here, she could see why. "How come there hasn't been much tourism until now? It's so incredibly beautiful."

The sun sparkled on the clear, shallow water. She could see the clean sandy floor below. A boat loaded with fresh-caught fish chugged by, heading for the quay.

"For so long, we had no hotels, no advertising, an obscure language that no one speaks." He glanced at her, sun dancing in his dark eyes. "Much as it pains me, I suspect the average person still isn't even aware Caspia exists."

He turned to stare at a white-sailed yacht cruising nearby. "Tessa, does that man look familiar?"

She squinted against the high sun and looked at a tall, tanned man with salt-and-pepper hair in a yellow polo shirt. She recognized his face from the TV news. "It looks like Senator Kendrick. What would he be doing here?"

Sebastian grabbed a pair of binoculars out of a compartment under the seat. "I thought so. He used to live in my building." He leaned over the side of the boat. "Michael! Charmaine!"

He spoke rapidly in Caspian to the boatman, who steered in their direction. Within minutes, Sebastian was helping Tessa up the ladder into the Kendricks' yacht.

Sebastian kissed them on both cheeks and introduced her. Nervous, she babbled that she was his assistant visiting from New York.

"I can't believe you came to Caspia without letting me know," Sebastian chided gently.

"We didn't really plan our visit," Mrs. Kendrick explained. "Michael decided to surprise me with a whirlwind tour of the Mediterranean to celebrate our thirtieth wedding anniversary."

Thirty years? Tessa hoped she looked that good ten years from now. Charmaine Kendrick's short, blond hair swept back to reveal an alert face. Her rose-colored shorts showed off fit, tanned legs.

"And naturally we couldn't sail right past Caspia," cut in the senator. "Not after you've sung its praises to us so often."

"You can see I wasn't exaggerating." Sebastian had his arm around both of them. "I'll be deeply offended if you won't join us at the palace for lunch."

Mrs. Kendrick brightened at this suggestion, but her husband quashed it with the explanation that they had a strict itinerary to stick to.

"Twenty ports in twenty days." Charmaine laughed. "We're expected in Piraeus tomorrow morning."

"What can I show you of Caspia while you're here? The ancient market? The early Christian frescoes? The Ottoman mosque?"

Tessa's ears pricked up. She silently voted for the frescoes.

Mrs. Kendrick shielded her eyes from the sun with a manicured hand. "Oh, my goodness, does that sign say Dolce & Gabbana?"

"It does." Sebastian grinned. "And that's BCBG Max Azria right next to it. How about some shopping?"

The senator clapped Sebastian on the back. "Charmaine never says no to shopping."

"Well, dear, we do have a lot of functions to go to. And I didn't realize it would still be so warm at this time of year."

"And scanty evening wear is something *I* never say no to." Senator Kendrick's tanned face eased into a grin.

The senator begged off going ashore with them and asked Tessa to keep him company while Sebastian took Mrs. Kendrick to the stores in his gondola.

Tessa didn't mind. She'd rather sit on a yacht and watch the water than shop any day. And if she remembered right, Senator Kendrick was a keen supporter of spending for education, a cause she held dear.

He guided her to the front of the yacht, where two padded seats looked out over the prow. She eased herself in next to him.

"So, you're Stone's assistant?"

"Yes." She turned to Kendrick with a smile. "I'm here to organize a meeting."

"Working for royalty must be rather bizarre for a girl used to American democracy." He puffed his athletic chest inside his lemon polo shirt.

"It was a bit strange at first, but I don't think much about it. The people of Caspia seem very content with their royal family."

"I don't suppose they have much choice." Senator Kendrick leaned in. His grin gave her a close-up of his blazing white teeth. There was something weird about his skin. Smooth and shiny, it looked like the skin of someone who'd had dermabrasion to erase wrinkles.

She looked over to the quay, where Sebastian was helping Mrs. Kendrick out onto the stone sidewalk that flanked the row of luxury boutiques.

"You're a quiet one, aren't you?"

"I guess I'm just dazzled by the view."

His pale blue eyes fixed on hers. "I'm rather dazzled by it myself."

Something about the way he stared at her made Tessa's stomach tighten.

"Too much foreign food and foreign scenery makes me pine for a little taste of home." He leaned in so close that his freckled arm brushed against hers. Her hairs stood on end.

She forced a laugh. "You're craving corn dogs and apple pie?"

"Something like that. I bet you're tired of being hit on by swarthy Mediterranean men."

"Not at all. The Caspians I've met have been very polite and charming."

"Carrying a torch for your prince, are you?" Senator Kendrick's salt-and-pepper eyebrow lifted.

"What?"

"I suppose all silly young girls fill their heads with fantasies of crowns and coronets. An American senator has a good deal more power than a tin-pot monarch."

"I imagine that's a matter of opinion."

Her stomach knotted. It would be tough to swim for shore in the long dress. She'd lost sight of Sebastian, too. He'd gone into one of the shops.

She decided to redirect the conversation. "What do you think about mandatory school testing? Do you think it ensures an even playing field, or do you think it makes teachers gear lessons too much toward the tests?"

Senator Kendrick threw his head back and guffawed with laughter. "I came here to get away from all that claptrap and political bull. Now I'm sailing on a boat with a beautiful blonde and she wants to bend my ear about education? I feel as if I'm back in New York."

The disgust in his voice made her eyes widen. She thought she caught a whiff of something on his breath, too. Whiskey?

She gathered her skirt about her knees and groped for a good excuse to leave the intimate seating.

"Where do you think you're going?"

"I'd like to take a walk on the deck."

"It's a small yacht. There's barely room to take three steps." His pale eyes narrowed. He leaned over her and trapped her with his arm by placing his hand on the armrest on the far side of her. "I can think of some far more interesting things to do."

He's going to kiss me.

The thought rushed Tessa's brain as his pursed lips rushed her mouth.

Instinct kicked in. Since she couldn't pull back, she whipped forward and smashed him in the nose with her forehead. She was on her feet and back on the deck in seconds. A young male sailor knelt nearby, winding some rope.

Senator Kendrick appeared around the sail, rubbing his nose. He glared at her. "Don't get the wrong idea."

"Don't worry, I didn't." She stood with her hands on her hips.

Now that her adrenaline was flowing she'd like him to try that again. She'd enjoy pitching him into the drink.

Maybe he read her mind, because he disappeared down some stairs into the belly of the boat.

She dusted her hands, which felt oddly satisfying. Hopefully her forehead wouldn't bruise. What a jerk! Did he think she'd *want* to kiss him?

She suspected he didn't spare a thought for what she wanted. She was a nobody. An assistant. A pretty, empty-headed bimbo to toy with.

The disturbing part was that she didn't want to tell Sebastian. He was obviously pleased to have important American visitors come to his country and she didn't want to spoil it for him.

It seemed an eternity before Sebastian finally appeared, his gondola laden with shiny bags from the boutiques.

Sebastian was all smiles as he helped Charmaine Kendrick back onto the boat. Tessa's heart squeezed with pity for the woman married to such a—

Now, now. She was the assistant to a prince. Nice girls didn't use words like that.

The senator—and she used the word loosely—must have been watching from below, because he came on the deck as soon as they arrived. He marched right past Tessa without looking at her.

"Did you buy some beautiful things, my dear?" He kissed his wife's cheek. "You know I want you to have everything your heart desires."

To make up for your cheating louse of a husband. Tessa could barely keep a straight face. Just the sight of the man made her flesh crawl.

"Tessa." Sebastian's voice in her ear made her jump. "Are you okay?" He murmured it low.

"Sure. I'm fine." Her attempt at bright and breezy came out rather stiff.

Sebastian shot a glance at the senator, who was "oohing" over some shimmery red number his wife pulled from a striped bag. "Seriously, you don't look yourself." His dark eyes filled with concern as he looked at her again.

Her stomach tangled. Should she tell him?

For all she knew her revelation might start an international incident. And she didn't want anything else to spoil this beautiful day. She was pretty sure the senator would turn tail and run as soon as she and the prince left the boat.

"I guess I don't have my sea legs yet." She glanced at the mirror-calm water of the harbor and swallowed.

"In that case, we must get you back on solid ground."

Senator Kendrick clapped a jovial hand on Sebastian's shoulder. Was his nose looking a tad swollen? "As I said, we've got a full itinerary. Our captain informed me that we must set sail before noon or we'll never make Piraeus in time."

He shot an icy glance at Tessa. She lifted her chin.

Yes. Definitely swollen. And a black eye seemed to be starting on the left side, too. Hah! Maybe he'd think twice before assaulting someone next time.

Sebastian kissed Charmaine on the cheek and made her promise to come back. Tessa was relieved she wouldn't be here when they did. She managed a curt goodbye to the man who'd spoiled her perfect morning.

Back in the gondola, with Sebastian's big, protective presence beside her, she shivered with relief.

"Enough boating for you." He leaned over the side and trailed his fingers in the water. "Warm. Want to take a dip?"

"Right here?" Panic crept over her. "I don't have a swimsuit with me."

"You didn't bring one at all?"

"No. I came here to study the files and help with the meeting, remember?"

"Oh, yes. That." He seemed to have genuinely forgotten. His eyes brightened. "We must find you a suit immediately."

He murmured instructions to the boatman. Spoken fast, the language was much harder to understand. She did catch the word *Valentino*.

"I don't need a Valentino swimsuit," she protested. "Is there an ordinary clothes store where I could find a suit?"

"What's wrong with Valentino?" He raised a brow.

"It's outrageously expensive, that's what."

Being a prince clearly made you lose touch with reality. Which probably didn't much matter if you were a prince.

She, however, had to save for the down payment on the apartment she'd be renting in LA. Patrick hadn't yet mentioned cohabiting and she'd decided it would be tacky and pushy to suggest it.

They could work up to that.

She wouldn't tell Patrick about the senator, either. He'd probably think she'd been dressed too provocatively or something.

"Beautiful things are always expensive. It's the way of the world." Sebastian eased his broad shoulders against the velvet seat.

"No, they're not." She sat up. "Usually things that cost nothing are the most beautiful." She looked up to where the sun illuminated the rocky peaks that stood sentinel over the town. "Does the blue sky cost money? The clear water? The fresh air?"

She paused. Perhaps there were cleanup crews constantly at work scrubbing and whitewashing Caspia.

"The sun in your golden hair."

Sebastian's low voice caught her off guard.

"What?"

"Beautiful." His eyes were narrowed, seductive.

Heat swelled in her chest, then morphed into a clench of anxiety. Was she inadvertently sending out some signal that she was interested or available?

She crossed her arms over her chest. "For all you know it costs a fortune to get my hair this color."

"Does it?" He looked curious.

She laughed again. "No. It's naturally a dark, mousy blond."

"It's perfect. And the Caspian sun admires it as much as I."

For a second she thought he was going to weave his fingers into her hair again. Her body braced in a mixture of terror and anticipation.

The boat bumped gently against the quay.

The boatman lashed the long boat to a metal ring set in the giant stones.

Tessa gathered her long dress and climbed out of the yawing boat with as much dignity as possible. The ancient stone buildings stood shoulder to shoulder along a stone walkway, inlaid with mosaic. She noticed small, tasteful signs above some of the doorways. "Chanel, Ferragamo, Armani."

"All the stores we've been working with."

He linked his arm though hers. She had to admit that his strong arm felt wonderfully supportive after what she'd just been through with a man she once respected. Sebastian would never take advantage of a vulnerable woman.

Not unless she wanted him to.

Now that she'd seen the Kendricks' white yacht leave through the harbor mouth, she started to relax, caressed by gentle sea breezes and the bright sun.

Inside Valentino, Sebastian addressed the fawning male clerk. "We'd like to see some swimsuits."

"Bikini or one-piece?"

"Bikini," Sebastian said firmly, before she'd managed to get her mouth open. The clerk hadn't even glanced at her. She wasn't sure he was even aware of her standing there, next to His Royal Highness.

"That's the one." Sebastian pointed to a greenish suit, four microscopic triangles held together by gold rings.

Tessa tilted her head. "Are you sure that's not a pair of earrings?"

Sebastian chuckled. "Try it on. If it doesn't fit the rest of you, we'll hang it from your ears."

Reluctant, she took the hanger and followed the clerk into a changing room. Thick carpet greeted her feet as she slipped off her sandals behind a heavy curtain. Was she supposed to go out and show Sebastian the bikini?

There was no mirror in the curtained cubicle, so she had to creep out into the main dressing room to confront her almost-naked body in a wall of mirrors.

She approached the mirror carefully, expecting an eyeful of skinny-and-pale.

"Very nice."

Sebastian's deep voice made her jump. She spun around to see him standing by the entrance to the dressing rooms, arms crossed and a smile of appreciation sneaking across his arrogant mouth.

"I could use a tan."

"Then the sooner we get out in the sun, the better." His smile became a broad grin. He held out his arm. "Let's go."

She laughed. "I have to get dressed again. And pay. This scrap of fabric is probably two hundred dollars."

He smiled wryly. "I've already paid. Here's the matching sarong." He handed her a shimmering piece of green-and-gold fabric.

Their hands brushed as she took it from him. A swift touch that made her heart beat faster.

For all she knew it was actually five hundred dollars and the sarong twice as much.

She sucked in a breath.

Eek. This was all a bit much.

It wasn't appropriate to let her boss dress her up like a Barbie doll. Especially when she was practically engaged to someone else.

Thoughts of Patrick seemed rather out of place here in Caspia. He didn't like hot sun and he'd be bored on the water. When they'd gone sailing out of Westport with one of his clients, he'd kept flipping on his PDA to check stock quotes.

Very practical. Sensible. The kind of person who'd make a responsible husband and father. So she'd better make sure she kept Patrick—and her own future—foremost in her mind.

Five

White liveried servants brought Tessa and Sebastian a lunch of handmade delicacies on the private palace dock. Hidden from the world by carved stone walls, they sipped fresh lemonade with sprigs of fragrant mint while seawater lapped at the sun-bleached quay. Bright flowers bloomed in ornate urns, their leaves occasionally ruffled by the warm breeze.

Tessa wriggled, trying not to get too comfortable on the soft lounge chair. She wore the bikini. She could hardly refuse when he'd sunk so much money into it.

"I really should call the attendees for the meeting."

"Not yet. You need heliotherapy." Sebastian picked up the hem of his shirt and pulled it over his head in a quick motion.

She jerked her gaze away from the sight of his bronzed washboard abs.

"Helio-what?" She fixed her attention on a seagull, then quickly became dizzy as it turned in tight circles, scanning the water for its lunch.

Sebastian was stretching. She could tell without looking.

Her nerve endings could see him. All the tiny invisible blond hairs all over her. Her nipples must be looking, too, because they buzzed like pressed doorbells.

"Heliotherapy. Sunlight as a curative. Practiced in Caspia since the time of Hippocrates."

She couldn't manage to avert her eyes as he eased back into his chair, settling his broad shoulders into the soft fabric.

A narrow cyclone of black hair started between his well-developed pecs, twisted down the center of his rock-hard stomach, then disappeared below the button of his black trunks.

"I thought…" Her voice was a hoarse whisper. She cleared her throat. "I thought the sun gave you skin cancer."

Sebastian snorted. "Caspians have the longest lifespan of any people on earth." He lifted his arms behind his head, and his impressive biceps bulged.

Tessa blinked.

"Well, you have pretty dark skin." All over. At least the parts she could see. She tried not to think about the others.

"So did you last summer. Have you been living under a rock this year?"

She couldn't help laughing. "I have, lately. The rock of Caspia Designs and its gritty financials."

Sebastian turned his head and assaulted her with one of his penetrating stares. "And that is exactly why I won't have you scurrying off to bury yourself again."

His eyes grazed her face, then wandered over her neck.

"You need sun, good food, fresh air and laughter. Then you won't want to run away to California in search of things that can be found right where you are now."

He settled his head back with a smile of satisfaction and closed his eyes.

He'd noticed her tan last summer?

She'd managed a large group plot in a local community garden, which kept her outdoors digging, weeding and watering at least an hour a day.

She'd had a great time, too. Hadn't spent one single evening sighing over her lack of husband prospects or her ticking biological clock.

This year she hadn't the time or energy for the garden. So she'd also missed out on the companionship, sunshine, fresh air and fresh food that came along with the experience.

Instead she'd been telling herself things would get better once she left New York and started over.

Maybe Sebastian had a point.

A self-protective urge to argue with him tickled her vocal cords. But he looked so peaceful and contented lying there in the sun. She didn't want to be snotty and point out that the older citizens of Caspia were pretty leathery looking.

Besides, she liked leather.

Still, sunblock would be a good idea. She fished the bottle from her bag and started to rub it on her exposed belly.

"Let me help."

She glanced up to see Sebastian's winning smile again. The one that made her so suspicious of his motives.

She fought the urge to laugh. "That's okay, I've got it covered."

"Not yet, you haven't. I'll do your back." He took the bottle from her in a firm swipe. "Turn around."

She turned, swinging her legs to the other side of the lounger. "Are you this commanding with people who aren't your employees?"

"I prefer to think of myself as straightforward."

His hands settled on her shoulders.

One way to be straightforward.

Breath rushed out of her lungs at the sensation of his broad fingertips, moist with lotion, rubbing her skin. He smoothed the sunblock over the nape of her neck, feathering it over her vertebrae with little thumb motions. She curled her toes, trying to fight the warm pool of arousal spreading in her abdomen.

His broad palms swirled lotion over her shoulder blades, kneading her muscle at the same time. It was hard to ignore the sensation of release spreading through her.

Then his fingers slid under the scanty string of her bikini. She gasped. For some reason the gesture seemed shockingly intimate.

"Hold still. I need more lotion." His voice was unusually gruff. She felt quite naked as he pulled his hands from her body.

She heard him rubbing the sunblock between his hands to warm it, and her skin tingled in anticipation of his touch.

Ooh. Right there in the sensitive spots on either side of her waist. She tried not to wriggle. Or giggle.

His fingers slid around to rub it over her belly button. She should protest that she could do that herself, but she'd lost the power of speech.

Probably because in reaching forward to rub her front, Sebastian had moved so close that she could smell his stirring male scent.

"Relax," he commanded. "Why are you tightening up?"

Um, because my boss is rubbing my bare flesh with his fingers?

She managed to clear her throat. "Guess I'm over-worked. Must be my demanding boss."

"I'll have a word with him."

She could hear the smile in his voice.

He pushed his fingers into the tight muscle on either side of her spine, causing her to arch her back and let go a tiny moan of pleasure.

"Ah, yes."

"What?" she croaked.

"I can see the problem."

"What problem?" Ohhhh. His thumbs settled into the dimples above her bikini bottom. That felt…wicked.

"You need to let go of *all* tension."

"I think I'm pretty close."

"No. Your muscles are still working to hold you up-right." His palms rubbed the sides of her waist. There wasn't even a hint of lotion left on them. Ripples of sensation skittered over her.

"Let me guess, you want me to lie down."

"No."

He didn't stop kneading the muscles behind her hips. She craned her neck around to read his expression.

His dark eyes flashed mischief. "I want you to float."

Sebastian lifted her off her chair before she could draw breath to protest. He held her in his arms, and for a second she thought he was going to heave her right into the water lapping against the stone quay.

Instead he marched to the edge, and jumped.

She let out a piercing scream as they plummeted through the air for a split second before splashing into the water. Tessa managed to close her mouth before they plunged below the blue-green surface into the silent world below.

Eyes shut tight and Sebastian's strong arms still tight around her, she surfaced, gasping for breath. "What the—"

"Now relax."

"Relax? You've half drowned me!" She struggled, trying to get free of his arms.

She looked up at his face as he brushed a strand of hair off her cheek. His expression was serious, his touch deft and careful.

Then their eyes met and her stomach did a weird leaping thing.

Being held close against his warm, wet chest felt anything but safe.

He trod water, holding them both up. His powerful legs created a swell, while his embrace seemed effortless, and strangely soothing.

"Let your legs float. I won't let go. I promise."

His deep voice tickled her wet ear.

She fought the ripple of pleasure it summoned. "Why would I believe you after you already dunked me?"

"The Caspian royal family never breaks a promise. Our motto is Honor Omnia Vincit."

"Honor conquers all, huh?"

"Engraved on my heart."

He flexed a brawny bicep in her face. There, scrolled into the pattern winding over his arm, were the words he'd spoken.

She tried to brush off the sensations sneaking through her. "I've got news for you. Your heart isn't really on your sleeve. It's an expression."

Sebastian's mouth creased into a smile. "Maybe I should dunk you." He dipped her a couple of inches.

Her stomach tightened, then softened when he brought her gently back to the surface. Water played over her stomach, echoing the ripple of arousal inside it. "It's a beautiful tattoo. Does every man in the family get one?"

Sebastian glanced down at it. The pattern of stylized leaves traced the swell of his muscles to ring his upper arm just below the shoulder. "I've had it so long I forget it's there. But no, it's not traditional." His eyes sparkled with humor. "My mom almost died when she saw it. I got it when I was sixteen after I went to an Eric Clapton concert in London with some friends."

Tessa laughed. "That's such a…regular guy thing to do."

"Who says I'm not a regular guy, as well as a prince?" He raised a brow.

Somehow that stopped her in her tracks. Not that she was making any tracks, since Sebastian still held her fast in his arms and her feet bobbed near the surface of the water. Royal trappings aside, Sebastian *was* just a guy. With a mind and heart and feelings. Like everyone else.

Like her.

She ignored the funny sensation in her gut. "It's lucky I was always strapped for cash as a teen or I might have the New York Knicks emblazoned on me somewhere. What made you decide to get the family motto?"

Sebastian looked at the scrolled words. "Caspia and its people are my team. I might have occasionally cheered for, say, Manchester United, but my heart is always in Caspia, and as you've observed, I wanted to wear it on my sleeve. Still do."

His eyes shone with a mix of passion and humor that made her heart squeeze.

How had their relationship gone overnight from five years of formal and professional relations to half-naked conversations and underwater encounters?

In some ways it was her wildest fantasy come true. The man she'd admired and mooned over for so long was actually teasing and flirting with her. It was hard not to be flattered.

And excited.

Sebastian adjusted his grip, sliding his strong arms under her. "Let your head rest. Let go. The water will carry you."

"I think you're doing most of the work."

"I wouldn't call it work." His deep voice had a playful tone.

But what was he playing at? They both knew this flirtation couldn't go anywhere. Not anywhere sensible, at least.

She shot him a challenging glance. "Me, either. I have phone calls to make."

"First you must heal and recover. Hydrotherapy has been recognized for thousands of years as a powerful curative." He shifted one of the hands supporting her torso and splashed a few drops of water on her hot skin.

She swallowed hard, trying to crush the sensations swelling inside her. "You should open a spa. Ancient healing therapies seem to be a specialty of yours."

"Excellent idea. Why didn't I think of that? See how valuable you are to me?"

"Oh, stop it."

"Stop what?" His expression was all innocence.

"Buttering me up so I'll stay and work for you."

Or do whatever else it is that you have in mind.

"Can you blame me?"

"Well, no. I am efficient and organized." She raised a brow. "And I do my best to present a professional appearance. Though that seems to have fallen by the wayside today…" She glanced at her bare stomach. Drops of seawater sparkled on skin that had already started to tan. A result of Sebastian's unthorough sunblock application.

What was he doing with his fingers? The pads of his fingertips played her waist like a piano, dancing over her until her insides hummed like vibrating strings.

Her nipples poked against the fabric of her scanty top. Heat and moisture gathered between her thighs, making her glad her bikini bottom was already damp.

Sebastian lowered his head so that his breath heated her ear. "As you point out, you are perfect. Which is exactly why you can't leave. I won't let you."

She shivered, the force of his words sinking in.

I don't want to leave.

She writhed slightly, trying to regain control of her body. The sensations swimming through her were startling and unfamiliar. Warm water swirled around her while the breeze tickled her bare skin above it. Sebastian's powerful hands held her crushed against his muscled chest. His musky scent wound through the salty tang in the air, threatening to overwhelm her senses.

Suddenly she was panting, gasping for breath, struggling against the firm hold of Sebastian's arms and the ache of her unwelcome arousal. "I have to stand!" She shoved against him with her elbow.

"It's too deep."

Flailing in the water, she started to panic. Frantic kicking had freed her from Sebastian, but now, head reeling and body throbbing, she couldn't seem to remember how to swim.

"It's okay, Tessa, I won't let you sink." Sebastian took her hand and tugged her gently to the stone dock. He didn't try to grab or control her, just guided her through the water. She grabbed a metal ring and clung to it.

She blew out a sharp blast of air. "I'm sorry. I guess it was all too much. I'm not cut out to be relaxed. It freaks me out."

Sebastian's look of concern eased into a grin. "You're a real New Yorker. You'd rather resist than relax."

"I'm from Connecticut," she protested.

"Same thing."

"No, it isn't."

"See, you want to fight me already."

"I do not!" She shifted her grip on the ring. How had this man managed to so thoroughly unhinge her?

"Oh, yeah?" He shoved his hand in the water and splashed her. Hard.

She splashed back and kicked with her feet, showering him completely with water until he ducked below the surface.

He rose up, laughing. "See what I mean?"

She shoved another wave of water at him. Damn. He was right. She felt better already.

She could even stare right at his handsome face with the water streaming over its hard lines and feel…almost normal.

"Do you surrender?" she challenged.

"Caspians never surrender."

"Honor Omnia Vincit, and all that." Her eyes wandered to the tattoo circling his thick bicep.

"Exactly. And since I am a man of honor, I'll help you out of the water. I think we've both had enough hydrotherapy for one afternoon." His black hair hung in his eyes, dripping with water.

He looked very unroyal.

And devastatingly handsome.

"It's okay. I can swim. I grew up in a coastal town. In *Connecticut.*" She dodged his offered hand and darted around him, diving under and pulling hard for the stone steps twenty feet along the dock.

As she climbed out of the water she sensed his eyes on her. She adjusted her scanty bikini, not that it made much difference. His steady dark gaze threatened to evaporate the water right off her.

This was *so* wrong.

A strange noise pierced the air. It took her a full five seconds to realize it was her cell phone. She dived for it, dragging her sarong over her bare legs.

Patrick. His work number. He'd called three times this morning just to "see how she was."

How could she talk to him now, while her inside pulsed with desire for another man?

Guilt speared through her as she pushed the button to send him straight to voice mail.

"*Now* can we see the files? I'm kind of a workaholic, so I get neurotic if I'm not allowed to work."

"You are working. You are my assistant and you are assisting me in enjoying my day." His arrogant expression dared her to argue.

She fought the urge to laugh. Obnoxious jerk!

And he was right, too, which made it worse.

She sucked in a deep breath and tried to compose herself. All she had to do was survive her two weeks' notice without doing anything stupid, then she could get on with the rest of her life.

"Do you have jeans?" His question yanked her back to the present.

"Yes."

"Great."

He shrugged his white linen shirt back on, right over his wet skin. It clung to his ripped chest in a very disturbing way. She was still attempting to tear her gaze from the sight when he looked up. "What are you waiting for?"

"What am I supposed to be doing?"

"Getting your jeans."

"Oh."

Sebastian looked at her as if she'd lost a cog or two. He was right. Of course, it was all his fault.

"I'll, uh, be right back." She strode into the palace, hoping she could find her way to her room.

In the wide, colonnaded hallway she passed the queen, who was talking at top speed on a cell phone. Despite her damp and seminaked appearance, Tessa prepared her brightest smile. Her Royal Majesty glanced up but didn't make any acknowledgment.

Ouch.

What did she expect? She was Sebastian's assistant, not a visiting princess. *Get over yourself already.*

Six

Sebastian drove through the gates that kept the rest of Caspia outside the palace walls. He negotiated his Land Rover through the narrow cobbled streets with expert ease, pausing for an occasional chat through the window.

"I think it's really nice that the royal family is so intimate with the people," Tessa remarked. She thought, too, that Sebastian seemed more relaxed here than in New York. There he often looked tense and rushed.

"Ha. It drives my mother crazy. She prefers to maintain a majestic distance. But my dad and I like people too much. We couldn't be cool and distant if we tried."

He leaned out the window to beckon a flower seller, then exchanged one of Caspia's large, colorful banknotes for a ribbon-tied bunch of pink, bell-shaped flowers.

He handed it to Tessa.

Now he was giving her flowers?

"Smell them."

She wanted to laugh. Typical of Sebastian to buy her flowers then order her to smell them.

She buried her nose in the soft petals. "Mmm. They smell like honey."

"Our Caspian honey smells like these flowers. It's the most delicious honey in the world."

"Of course it is." She grinned. "Is there anything in Caspia that isn't the best in the world?"

Sebastian turned to her—while continuing to speed along a windy, narrow stretch of road—and gave her an incredulous look. "You've spent a day here. Surely you know the answer to that already." He faced front again and she loosened her grip on the door handle. "We're headed for the place where these flowers grow, in the cool and shady crevices of our mountains."

"Let me guess, they're the most beautiful mountains in the world?"

Sebastian stared straight ahead as he drove. "You're catching on."

The Land Rover climbed toward the sky, bumping along a narrow, unpaved track. Grasses and wildflowers grew sparser as they rose through the rugged terrain, past the occasional grazing goat.

When it seemed as if surely they'd scrape the roof of the car on the hovering white clouds, he screeched to a stop in a cloud of dust.

"Jump out."

She did. And it was quite a jump, onto loose shale. She skidded then got her footing on the desolate crag they'd ascended. She was about to make a crack along the lines of "where's the royal pavilion?" when she looked up and the view made words shrivel on her tongue.

The land descended right from her toes in a sweeping cascade of rock, grass and flowers still brilliant in the dusk. A wide plain of grazed meadows punctuated the dramatic slope, then the land descended again to the city, where the red clay roofs of the ancient buildings hugged the hillside as it ringed the harbor.

"We're two thousand feet above sea level."

The ocean, far below, crinkled and twinkled in the setting sun. She could make out the dots of bright colored fishing boats returning to the harbor, and others setting out for the night's catch.

Smoke rose from chimneys, no doubt rich with the aroma of Caspian dinners being cooked.

The lowering sun just touched the wide, dark sea, a bright orb that bathed land and water in transparent golden light.

It was so beautiful Tessa could hardly breathe.

"Now you've truly seen Caspia. This is our whole nation."

Sebastian's deep voice drew her gaze from the view. His pride and emotion were written plainly on the strong features of his face.

He stared at her. His gaze heated her face, but she couldn't find words to cut through a new tension that thickened the air.

He reached out and again he played with her hair. She couldn't move. Her synapses crackled as excitement rushed through her.

The golden light burnished Sebastian's complexion to a warm bronze, making him more handsome than ever—

like a prince from an ancient myth, here to rescue her from the humdrum reality of life and transport her to…

Somewhere like this.

"She must have looked like you." His words were almost a whisper. His fingers roamed in her hair as his gaze wandered over her face and neck.

"Who?" She tried to ignore the hum of arousal vibrating through her.

"The golden statue."

"The one that used to stand in the harbor?" Tessa squinted at him. She expected to see his face crease into a laugh, but it didn't.

"Yes." He tilted his head and gazed into her eyes. "The ancient statue of Andara that used to watch over our bay. The guardian of the people of Caspia."

He paused and his eyes narrowed. "Now that I see you here, with your bright hair streaming in the breeze and the sun on your golden skin, I can picture her perfectly."

Embarrassed, Tessa pushed a stray hair off her face. She could feel heat rising to color her cheeks. "I'm glad sunset in Caspia suits me, but I'm just Tessa from Connecticut. Trust me on this."

His eyes held hers, unblinking. "Tessa from Connecticut, you are the most beautiful woman I've ever seen."

He spoke with such conviction that the breath crept out of her lungs.

Then a shard of good sense peeked through the sudden fog of desire: *This is Sebastian Stone, world famous seducer.*

"You're not bad yourself, in the right light." She tried to laugh, but no sound came out.

She stood transfixed by the hot gaze of his dark eyes. Something in her said "run!" but she didn't move a muscle.

Then he stepped forward and pressed his lips to hers in a swift motion that almost buckled her knees.

His hard torso brushed her breasts, tightened her nipples into peaks. He gathered her into his arms, his strong hands covering her back as he pulled her closer.

Gentle at first, his kiss deepened, becoming forceful, intense. A current of heat seared her as his tongue touched hers.

His rough cheek against her own sun-heated face roused her senses. He smelled like sun and earth and salt air—not the things you'd expect a prince to smell like— but magic, and she couldn't help but respond.

Her arms slid around his waist, against the hard muscle of his back. He groaned as his pelvis bumped against hers. The rough denim of his jeans chafed her. She wanted to slide his jeans down over his powerful thighs and...

Tessa! The shocking thought tugged her out of the haze of raw, pulsing lust that deprived her of her common sense.

What were they doing?

Well...right now Sebastian was devouring her neck, his mouth hungry and unforgiving, his teeth scraping deliciously against the ultrasensitive area behind her ear.

And she was moaning... Or would that sound be better described as whimpering?

Stop!

The word formed in her brain, then dissipated into a fog of desire as Sebastian took her mouth again in a hot, un-relenting kiss.

She didn't want to stop. Not at all. The sensations pouring through her like thick honey made her want to beg for more.

So what if he was her boss?

If he was a prince?

If he only wanted her for one hot, raw, ravenous night?

She shivered, her desire for him almost too much to bear.

Her fingers clawed at his shirt, then reached under it to touch his hot, hard muscle. She ground her hips against his and he responded, molding himself to her.

Her breasts crushed against his chest, her nipples thick with sensation as he hiked up her shirt and slid his hand over her bare back.

Then Sebastian unbuttoned her shirt. Slowly, carefully, his big fingers handled the buttons with gentle care. He eased it down her arms.

Her own breaths were ragged and unsteady in the quiet dusk. She saw the last copper rays of the sun as it sank behind the sea, taking with it the heat and bustle of the day.

And leaving the rich, thick darkness of the night.

Through her bra Sebastian laved her nipple with his tongue. Sharp sensation skidded over her and she almost lost her footing. His quick hands and strong arms soon righted her. He held her steady, tight, as he lowered his mouth and sucked—hard—on her other nipple.

The rough gesture aroused her to the point of agony.

"Come." He took her hand.

His thick arm supported her across a patch of slippery shale and up the side of a rocky ledge.

He stepped through a narrow opening between two boulders and gestured for her to follow.

Tessa's legs shook under the weight of unfamiliar feelings and sensations, as she stepped through the rocky opening. Behind the rocks lay a flat patch of hilltop, lit only by a slim, crescent moon.

Soft, thick grass tickled the sides of her feet above her sandals.

High rocks hid them from everyone and everything but the slender moon. Sebastian pulled her close and she shivered as he wrapped his powerful arms around her and held her tight.

Being wrapped in Sebastian was perfect.

Too perfect.

"Um, what are we doing?"

"Right now, I'd say we're hugging." He nuzzled her neck.

Shimmers of sensation danced along her shoulder and cascaded over her torso.

Her unclothed torso. Her shirt was out there on the rock face, somewhere.

"And now...we're kissing." The end of the last word blurred as his lips settled over hers.

His tongue danced with hers, making her insides twist and untwist in a pulse of excitement.

Her breasts met the night air as her bra came unhooked. "And now I'm undressing you," he murmured, pulling back just enough to get the words out.

He slid her bra over her arms, his fingers gentle, his eyes hungry.

"Beautiful."

His words caressed her along with his touch.

She did feel beautiful right now. Couldn't help it, with Sebastian's warm, dark gaze heating her blood.

She lifted his shirt over his head, which took some help, as it didn't seem anxious to leave his thick muscles.

His torso shone like pewter in the scant moonlight, that line of dark hair twisting down into his jeans.

Jeans that bulged with arousal.

Tessa breathed out slowly, trying to keep a clear head as she unbuttoned the snap at his waist. He was hard as the rock they stood on. She reached in and took him in her hand, enjoying the force of his arousal, kissing him, breathing in the rich, male scent of him.

"Tessa." His throaty voice caressed her ear like a summer breeze.

She heard the snap of her own jeans, but barely felt them slide over her thighs and down her legs. Her whole body sang with so much sensation.

Sebastian rubbed his thumbs over her nipples, which stood to attention. Her belly shuddered as he pressed his thick erection into her soft flesh.

His thigh pressed between hers, rough denim against her bare skin. He grasped her backside and pulled her closer, higher, pressing her breasts against his chest and crushing her mouth to his until she thought she'd catch fire.

"Take them off," she breathed. Indelicate in her desperation, she shoved and pushed at the stiff fabric of his jeans. "Lie down."

She thought she saw the gleam of his grin in the dark as Sebastian lowered himself into the cool, soft grass. She tugged his jeans and he sprang free, then she pulled them down over his legs.

Wow.

Sebastian's muscled, athlete's body looked like an ancient statue come to life. And why wouldn't it? He was descended from the warriors and champions of the ancient world. The tribal tattoo on his arm only added to the effect.

His fierce arousal heated her blood as he rolled a

condom over it. She climbed over him, hungry for his hardness inside her.

Her hair brushed his chest as she took him deep. Her moan pierced the silent night air and made her open her eyes for a split second.

She saw darkness. Silence. The stars.

And Sebastian.

She couldn't stop now even if she wanted to.

Shivering with the force of her need, she rocked, drawing him deeper into her pulsing core.

Urgency kicked into a fierce rhythm, and she wasn't sure how much longer she could last without blasting out into the stars. Then Sebastian reversed their positions in a deft move that left him on top and her down in the soft grass.

She writhed under him, enjoying the contrast of his hot, hard body and the cool, yielding ground. Sebastian's hands roamed over her skin, squeezing and enjoying her body. He sucked her breasts and the skin of her neck until she cried out.

Deep inside her, his erection danced, stirring sensations she'd never experienced before. Never even imagined.

She couldn't stop moving, wriggling under him, pressing herself to him and shifting her hips against his, testing and enjoying each new wrinkle of pleasure and the fresh ache of raw passion.

Kissing was clearly Sebastian's first language. His kisses came in unending variety—soft and teasing, wicked and sly, rough and hungry; or slow, controlled and throbbing with reined-in desire.

Strange, new feelings built inside her, consuming her, taking her over like an invasion.

She exploded into climax totally without warning, pealing out a sharp scream that rang over the nation of Caspia, followed by a series of hard gasps as sensation racked her body.

Her nails clawed into Sebastian as his own climax shook him. Then he lowered himself to her, heavy and breathless. He pushed his hands into her hair, holding her, and he pressed his rough cheek to hers.

Emotion swelled inside Tessa. Sebastian was so passionate in every other part of his life, should she be surprised that his lovemaking reflected his nature?

Stars danced in front of her eyes and she wasn't sure if they formed part of distant solar systems or were the creations of her own bedazzled brain.

Sebastian eased himself off her and lay on the ground beside her, his arm wrapped around her chest.

She felt…protected. Cherished.

Not loved, though.

Even now she didn't delude herself, even for a split second, that Sebastian Stone, Crown Prince of Caspia, could love her.

Which was fine. Because she had…

Ohmigod. Patrick!

She tried to sit up, but Sebastian's arm was too heavy on her chest.

She'd just cheated on the man she planned to— potentially—spend the rest of her life with.

Horror descended over her like a bucket of cold water. She hadn't even thought of him. Hadn't cared at all about him.

His message was still flashing, unheard, on her cell phone.

She sank back into the grass, head pounding.

"You okay?" Sebastian's deep voice stirred a fresh pulse of arousal.

"Sure. Fine." She swallowed. "Great."

She spotted a torn condom packet lying in the grass. She'd been too carried away to think of practical things. She was on the pill—at Patrick's insistence—but Sebastian didn't know that. It was thoughtful of him to remember protection.

Naturally the notorious Prince of Midtown carried a ready supply wherever he went. Perhaps he'd planned this.

Tension tightened her muscles.

Sebastian propped himself on one elbow. Her resistance ebbed as he stroked her cheek with his thumb. "I like a woman who knows how to give orders."

Her eyes met his. Humor sparkled in his dark gaze.

"Orders? What do you mean?"

Sebastian laughed. "I guess you were so caught up in the moment, you don't remember commanding me to strip and lie down."

He brushed a kiss over her lips. They parted, as heat rushed through her, embarrassment mingling with unavoidable desire.

She bit her lip. "Did I really? I'm so sorry."

"Don't be." Sebastian's wide mouth turned up at the corners. "I loved it." He growled and nipped at her neck. "Why shouldn't you ask for what you want? That's the best way to get it."

He licked her lips and pressed his mouth over hers in a hot, raunchy kiss.

She couldn't resist twisting to crush her body against his, flesh against flesh, enjoying the heat and hard masculinity of him.

He pulled back for a moment to look at her. "Too many people drift through life, afraid to ask for what they want. Afraid to figure it out, even. I'm glad you're not like that, Tessa."

I'm not?

She blinked and shoved a hand through her hair—which was no doubt tangled and filled with bits of grass. "I'm not so sure I do know what I want."

She wanted change, for sure. A shake-up. New surroundings. New possibilities.

And here she was, naked in the arms of a royal prince, on a foreign mountaintop.

Apparently she'd succeeded. Though this was not exactly what she'd had in mind.

Sebastian brushed his lips over her forehead. "You knew exactly what you wanted a few minutes ago. And I suspect that a few minutes from now you'll have some more strong ideas on the subject."

His suggestive tone tugged at a knot of need deep inside her. His mouth followed the cord of arousal down her torso, sucking her breasts, feathering butterfly kisses on her stomach, until his head was buried between her legs, kissing and licking her into an alternate dimension.

"Don't stop!" Her hips bucked at the sensations roused by his lips and tongue. "Faster, harder."

Sebastian responded instantly to her rasped requests, driving her deeper and deeper into a dark oasis of pleasure that blotted out the moon and stars.

Then he was inside her again, turning her mind and body inside out in explosions of rapture and sheer, earth-shaking pleasure.

This time they came together. A perfectly orchestrated

explosion, controlled yet devastating, that left them clinging to each other, sweaty, ecstatic and gasping for breath.

Even when blood started to return to her brain, Tessa was unable to summon a lick of embarrassment.

Sebastian lay fast asleep, his face buried in her hair, hugging her like his favorite teddy.

And weirdly enough it felt totally natural and comfortable.

Although his princely upbringing had created a sense of entitlement that could make him seem brash or arrogant, Sebastian was an affectionate and giving person. Something obviously appreciated by the citizens of Caspia, his vast crowd of friends, and the hordes of beautiful women who flung themselves at him daily.

The same could not exactly be said for Patrick. He was nice, but in a shy, reserved, New England kind of way. You could call him standoffish.

No one would ever call Sebastian standoffish. If he had a standoff with anyone, it would be a colorful occasion worthy of a tabloid front page.

There were a few of those in the media file.

He lived every day, every hour, with passion.

He even slept with passion. She smiled as she saw the blissful expression on his handsome face, the rapid movements of his eyes under his closed eyelids.

Is he dreaming about me?

She cursed herself for the thought, but went back to it anyway. Maybe he was picturing her, all in gold, standing guard over the Caspian harbor.

Two hundred feet tall.

Telling him to get his clothes off. Now!

She chuckled. The subtle movement made Sebastian snuggle closer.

Oh, dear.

This was all a little too wonderful. She had that nasty sensation right before you rip off a Band-Aid.

The next part is going to hurt.

Seven

Sebastian woke Tessa with gentle kisses. He made love to her one more toe-curling time before they tugged their clothes on and drove back down the mountain, just in time to beat the dawn.

Tessa wished she could disappear as they steered past the palace guards at 5:00 a.m.

No prizes for guessing what we've been up to, she mentally told them.

Sebastian didn't seem the slightest bit put out.

Of course, he probably brought disheveled but satisfied women back to the palace at dawn quite often.

He did show some circumspection in guiding her through the halls. That was nice. She didn't want to run into either of their royal majesties until she'd managed to get the leaves out of her hair.

Then he kissed her good-night, with a provocative thrust of his tongue.

Oh, boy.

Tessa collapsed onto her bed in a puddle of dreamy lust.

"Good morning, Tessa." The queen looked up from a large newspaper, printed in French. "You look a bit flushed. Are you feverish?"

Tessa gulped. "I'm fine. Maybe I got a bit too much sunlight yesterday."

Or moonlight…

After only a few hours sleep she eased herself into her seat and spooned some yogurt and honey into a bowl. Once again she'd come to the table with shower-damp hair.

Sebastian whistled as he helped himself to a heaping portion of some kind of Caspian fish stew. For breakfast.

Tessa wanted to kick him under the table and tell him to look less exuberant. He was going to give the game away.

Perhaps he just didn't care?

He chatted with his father about fishing reports and a construction project in the hills, and regaled Tessa with tidbits and statistics about Caspia's economy.

Sebastian could be quite grumpy in the morning, especially before the vat of coffee—with the consistency of used motor oil—he needed to get his systems going.

Today he was downright bubbly even before his first sip. The king's bright eyes twinkled with good humor as Sebastian described the previous day's tour of Caspia. She could see where Sebastian got his natural joie de vivre.

His looks clearly came from his mother, a severe beauty with bone structure sharp as a deadly weapon. She chatted politely with Tessa, asking innocuous questions about her college studies and her life in New York, but she didn't have the warmth of the Stone men, and Tessa was glad when she swept off to some assignation.

Sebastian's father leaned back in his chair. She could swear he was giving her a once-over. It would be disconcerting if not for his good-natured expression. "Do you ride, Tessa?"

She hesitated. *Ride what? A bike?*

Sebastian took a swig of coffee. "He means a horse."

"Oh. Yes, actually I do."

Sebastian looked surprised. "I thought you were from the city."

"I learned in school. To be honest, I haven't ridden since then. So maybe I've forgotten how."

"Impossible." Sebastian rose and dropped his napkin on the table. "Gio, tell the stables to prepare Alto and Magna for us immediately."

Tessa's mouth dropped open. Her adrenaline surged. Was it fear of making an ass of herself on a horse she couldn't control? Or a rush of excitement at the prospect of riding a horse again after all these years?

Sebastian pulled out her chair as she stood. "Do you have riding clothes?"

She shot him a look that said *You're kidding, right?* Then remembering the king was watching, she said, "I'm afraid not."

Sebastian suppressed a snort of laughter at her attempted change of demeanor. "Don't worry. We'll find you some."

He whipped out his cell and murmured something in Caspian. When he hung up, he was beaming. "Caspia is never more beautiful than from the back of a horse."

* * *

Sebastian loved to gallop across the open grassy meadows that belted the middle of Caspia, between the high mountains and the city. It was even better with Tessa galloping like a gale at sea in front of him, her golden hair whipping about her shoulders.

It was all he could do to keep up, and his mount was usually the more spirited of the two.

Tessa Banks was something else.

"You learned how to ride at St. Peter's?"

She turned her horse in a fast circle and came up beside him. "Yup. I got a job grooming the other students' horses and the instructor was nice enough to give me some lessons."

Her white cotton shirt was damp with perspiration, and Sebastian admired the view of her dark bra underneath. He raised his gaze, not wanting to harden painfully against the pommel of his saddle.

"And soon I was exercising the horses, as well as grooming them." Her face shone in the midday sun, her color heightened by exertion.

He could swear on his life that he'd never seen a more beautiful sight.

Tonight she would glitter amongst the crowd at the benefit ball. He'd be the envy of every man in the room.

She patted her horse's neck. "This does beat filing."

He took a minute to process her words.

Oh, yes. She was his assistant.

He'd forgotten about that.

Still, no reason he couldn't escort her to the ball. She was his guest here, in addition to being an employee.

Awkward that he'd slept with her. He usually had strict

rules about that sort of thing, drummed into him with stern warnings by his mother, and gentler and more practical admonitions from his father.

So far, he'd kept the house rules.

But there was something about Tessa that made rules seem foolish and irrelevant.

"We must choose your gown." He let his eyes drift over her long, muscled body as it flowed with the horse's supple back.

"Gown? For what?"

"Tonight's ball for Harvest of Health. It's one of my mother's favorite charities. She's invited all the crowned heads of Europe."

Tessa eyes widened.

"It'll be fun. They're not all over seventy. You'll enjoy the dancing."

Tessa slowed her horse to a trot. Sebastian's own mount was so fired up it took Sebastian a moment to rein him in and trot back to her.

"I don't think I should, Sebastian." Her lovely face looked troubled. "Last night was…wonderful, but I don't want people to talk about me."

"Of course you do. If no one's talking about you, it means you're not having enough fun."

She laughed. "I'd rather live the kind of life that doesn't make the headlines."

Sebastian stiffened, which made his horse jump. By the time he had it going forward again instead of sideways, Tessa was walking along on her horse, looking ahead, as if he wasn't even there.

Why did it bother him that she didn't want the kind of life he led?

He was hardly planning to marry her.

His horse gave another leap sideways.

He turned him in a circle and stroked his neck.

Well, he wasn't.

From the corner of his eye he saw Tessa lean forward to brush a fly from her horse's mane. Like all her movements, the gesture was as elegant as a ballerina's arabesque.

A thick sensation crept across his chest, tightening it. He shook it loose with a jovial chuckle. "I probably should feel guilty about depriving Caspia Designs of your capable hands."

"But let me guess, you don't." She turned to him, her lovely face lit with a grin.

"Not in the least. Race you!"

He surged forward. Maybe exertion would burn off some of the adrenaline surging in his blood.

Alone in a palace hallway, Tessa tried to walk with as much dignity as possible. Her dress, picked out that afternoon at one of Caspia's chichi boutiques, clung to her body like sea spray. The fabric, beaded with a million tiny jade-colored beads, swung as she walked, shimmering with every movement.

Sebastian had talked her into it. At least wearing a dress this heavy probably counted as weight-bearing exercise.

Not that she needed any after galloping all over the countryside with Sebastian, then indulging in an afternoon of Sebastian-funded power shopping to "support the local economy."

Speaking of Sebastian, where was he?

From the cool solitude of the colonnaded hallway, Tessa

could hear a hum of voices, clinking glasses and tinkling laughter. With each step she took the din grew louder.

The ball.

Her stomach turned over.

She'd never been to a ball.

Although she went to a school where balls were a fairly common form of vacation pastime, she couldn't remember ever being invited to one.

No doubt her classmates—with that inimitable prep-school-bred radar that can distinguish "one of us" from "one of them"—had known better than to ask her. Thus avoiding all kinds of embarrassment of her not having the right clothes to wear, or the correct etiquette.

She'd managed to dodge the gaffes she was about to make right now.

"You look breathtaking."

Sebastian's voice in her ear was low and thick with admiration.

"Thanks," she managed.

"I've been waiting for you. I thought you might not want to walk in there alone."

His thoughtfulness warmed and soothed her anxious heart. "You're so right." She smiled. "I'm trying to walk without getting tangled in my dress."

His dark gaze swept along her legs. "I can see how that could be a problem. Your legs are very long."

"They used to call me Knitting Needles."

Did she have to tell him that?

One dark brow lifted. "Because your legs are so long?"

Her face heated. "Yes, and my mom was always knitting. She brought it with her everywhere. She used to knit through all my basketball games."

Shut your trap and stop babbling!

Sebastian's curious gaze deepened. "You played basketball?"

"What else would I do with a body like this?" She gestured at her too-long-and-tall physique, accidentally grazing her knuckles on the green beads.

The mellow hum of music and a hundred conversations swelled as they neared the large atrium where the party was taking place. She walked along the receiving line, shaking hands with the king and queen, despite the fact that she'd had breakfast with them that morning, then a liveried servant announced her name to the crowd.

These people loved ceremony.

"Sebastian, dahling!" An older woman with about a kilo of diamonds hanging from her neck stalked forward on spindly legs. "How lovely to see you. I can't believe we missed each other at Philip's shindig last month."

Sebastian murmured pleasantries.

Tessa's frontal lobes buzzed with the realization that Philip's shindig was that big party in Monaco during which Sebastian was photographed with no less than twelve different wealthy beauties.

The guy from the clipping service had even joked that Sebastian made every minute count.

"And this is Tessa Banks."

Tessa glanced at him, expecting him to add "my assistant." But he didn't.

The woman looked at her expectantly for a moment, then held out her bejeweled hand.

Tessa shook it.

"Charmed, my dear."

"Oh, me, too!" She swallowed. *Did she have no social graces whatsoever?* "It's a lovely night."

She could almost hear Sebastian laughing. But he had the decency to make it silent laughter.

He slid his arm around her back and drew her away. She tried not to get distracted by the warmth of his hard muscle, which was obvious even through his austere dark suit.

"She's harmless," he muttered. "Which is more than I can say for this one. Hello, Faris."

Tessa's shoulders tightened. She recognized the name. Faris Maridis was a frequent and impatient caller when Sebastian was in New York. He always took her calls.

A tall, black-haired woman in a dark blue dress swept toward Sebastian. She grabbed him by the shoulders and planted extravagant kisses on each tanned cheek, leaving moues of red lipstick.

Tessa fought the urge to whip out a tissue and wipe them off.

"You're so wicked, Sebastian darling! Why haven't you taken me out on the *Mirabella* yet?"

His new yacht. She'd seen the paparazzi pictures.

"I've been busy with the lovely Tessa." He gestured to her. Faris whipped around. She gave Tessa a glare that raised goose bumps, then morphed into a big, toothy smile.

"Tessa? I don't believe we've met. Oh, wait! You're Sebastian's little 'girl Friday,' aren't you?"

Tessa blinked. People didn't usually call you "little" when you were nearly 5'10".

"She's my right-hand woman." Sebastian clearly relished the description. As he said it, his arm slid protectively around her waist.

She softened under her bead-encrusted dress.

Faris's sharp dark eyes darted to Sebastian's gesture, then back up to Tessa. They narrowed. "Is this your first time in Caspia, Tessa?"

"Yes. Sebastian's been kind enough to show me almost every inch of it."

"Has he now?" She shot an icy smile at him. "Sebastian is always so *thorough* when he entertains guests." She tilted her head. Her black hair was slicked into a chignon pierced by a single black hairstick. "Especially female guests." She winked at him.

Tessa flushed. It didn't help that Sebastian squeezed her bottom gently at that exact moment. Her nipples tightened and heat gathered between her hips.

She struggled to keep a straight face.

What if someone saw?

"Faris is one of my *oldest* friends." Sebastian stared at her. "That's why she feels free to be so shockingly rude to me."

Faris looked startled and let out a hollow laugh. "Oh, Sebastian, you are too much. Shall we ride tomorrow?"

"I think the horses could use a day of rest after what Tessa and I put them through today." He smiled and squeezed Tessa again.

She tried not to fall off her spiky heels.

Faris's red lips pressed together. "Daddy said you're calling a meeting about Caspia Designs."

Sebastian stiffened. "Yes. Tessa's arranged a gathering of the board for next Tuesday."

"Daddy's rather bored playing golf every day. The firm was always sort of a pet project for him."

"I can tell," murmured Sebastian through gritted teeth. "It's time to take Caspia Designs in a new direction."

Faris raised a slim brow. "Don't forget, Daddy is your father's oldest friend."

That explains a lot. Tessa had wondered why the firm had been allowed to stagnate under incompetent management for so long. Uncollected debts, dwindling markets, exorbitant costs leading to tiny profits on even the most expensive items.

She jumped as the band struck up a fast-paced new tune and people started leaping around as if they had fire ants in their pants.

"Come." Sebastian grabbed her hand and pulled Tessa into the fray. "It's our national dance. You'll like it."

She wasn't sure if his last words were conviction based on personal knowledge of her, or a royal command. She decided to assume the latter.

Sebastian grabbed her hand and whirled her around, then they took off across the floor at a galloping pace in a kind of whirling polka.

Blasts of trumpet and the rolling thunder of drums filled the air with a steamroller of sound. Colors and lights flashed before her eyes as they whipped around the room. Sebastian's strong arms and capable guidance swept her into the dance as if she knew it.

By the time the trumpets subsided to a farewell hum, she was gasping for air and dying to do it again.

"See, I told you." Sebastian pushed a stray strand of hair behind her shoulder. His own black hair remained slicked into place. His stern features betrayed no emotion.

But something new and different sparkled in his dark eyes. She couldn't help a rush of excitement as he stared at her.

"That was fun."

NO POSTAGE
NECESSARY
IF MAILED
IN THE
UNITED STATES

BUSINESS REPLY MAIL
FIRST-CLASS MAIL   PERMIT NO. 717   BUFFALO, NY

POSTAGE WILL BE PAID BY ADDRESSEE

SILHOUETTE READER SERVICE
3010 WALDEN AVE
PO BOX 1867
BUFFALO NY 14240-9952

If offer card is missing write to: Silhouette Reader Service, 3010 Walden Ave., P.O. Box 1867, Buffalo, NY 14240-1867

Get FREE BOOKS and
FREE GIFTS when you play the...

LAS VEGAS
GAME

*Just scratch off
the gold box with a coin.
Then check below to see
the gifts you get!*

YES! I have scratched off the gold box. Please send
me my **2 FREE BOOKS** and **2 FREE GIFTS** for which I qualify. I
understand that I am under no obligation to purchase any
books as explained on the back of this card.

326 SDL ESTE   225 SDL ESWQ

FIRST NAME	LAST NAME

ADDRESS

APT.#	CITY

STATE/PROV.	ZIP/POSTAL CODE

(S-D-09/08)

7	7	7	Worth TWO FREE BOOKS plus TWO FREE GIFTS!
🍒	🍒	🍒	Worth TWO FREE BOOKS!
🔔	🔔	♣	TRY AGAIN!

www.eHarlequin.com

Offer limited to one per household and not valid
to current subscribers of Silhouette Desire®
books. All orders subject to approval.

The music slowed to a lilting dance number. Tessa wondered if they'd exit the floor. She should probably dash to the bathroom and make sure her makeup wasn't streaming down her face.

But Sebastian pulled her into his arms. "Don't even think of running off."

Tessa laughed. Partly to distract herself from the rather overwhelming sensation of being pulled close to Sebastian's broad chest.

His black suit had an unusual design, a sleek jacket with no lapels and a Nehru collar. Smooth black pants with no crease. Hip and modern, rather than classic and traditional.

The Caspian royal family apparently preferred clean designer lines to gold brocade and rows of medals.

But no amount of well-cut cloth could hide the brawny muscularity of Sebastian's athletic body.

The scent of him, musky and enticing, enveloped her as he held her close, swaying to the music.

"Where were we before we got so rudely interrupted?" His low voice tickled her neck. "Oh, yes. Basketball. High school or college?"

"Both. I got a scholarship to St. Peter's and another one to college. It's the only reason I was able to go to either of them."

"Your family isn't well-off?"

"Not like that. My dad had the same job for forty years. He made a living but not enough to send me to the ritziest school in New England."

"What did he do?"

"Custodial director. That's what he always called himself." She looked right at Sebastian. "At the high school."

His eyebrows lowered slightly in an expression of confusion. "Custodial director. Is that...? I mean, did he...?"

"Clean the school? Yes." It came out a little sharper than she'd intended. But she'd had this discussion before and it usually ended in raucous laughter and raised eyebrows and her never being treated quite the same again.

Which was fine. Better to know who will treat you fairly and with respect, and who won't.

She looked at him, ready to see laughter and derision in his eyes.

Instead she saw something very different.

Admiration.

She sucked in a breath and dragged her attention to the dancers behind her.

"I'm impressed." His deep voice tickled her ear. "Not only can you play basketball competitively, but you managed to negotiate the social jungle of two of the world's most exclusive schools."

"Oh, I don't know that I so much negotiated it as made my own way through with a hatchet." She raised an eyebrow.

He laughed. "I'd have liked to see that."

"It wasn't pretty."

"I guess that depends on your aesthetic." His dark eyes roamed over her face, and her skin heated under his appreciative gaze.

"I bet you fit right in with all those children of CEOs and foreign dignitaries." He tilted his head, stared right into her eyes. "You look like an aristocrat. An American princess."

Tessa burst out laughing. "What does an American princess look like?"

Sebastian's lips twitched as he tried to keep from smiling. "Majestic."

"Well, I guess you're an experienced judge so I'll have to take your word for it."

It was so easy to forget that Sebastian was one of the fabled Crowned Heads of Europe.

You'd expect a monarch—even a future one—to be starched and stodgy. To have clothes tailor-made on Jermyn Street, not in a Milan design atelier.

In his leisure time you'd expect him to wear an earth-toned Harris tweed jacket, not a black Dolce & Gabbana T-shirt that clung to his rippling muscles.

On the other hand, you might well expect a future king to spend his time traveling the world, dancing and yachting and riding and skiing and seducing beautiful women from every nation.

In that sense, Sebastian was every bit a traditional prince.

And she'd better not forget it.

Sebastian couldn't take his eyes off Tessa's lithe body as it moved beneath the subtle sparkle of her dress.

He couldn't take his hands off her, either.

Electricity crackled between them as he held her close in a slow dance hours later. He felt hot and he wished he could peel some clothes off.

But he was too well trained in Royal Dignity for that.

And there'd be plenty of time for peeling clothes off later. In fact, he was making very detailed plans to extract Tessa's gorgeous glowing body—inch by inch—from her slinky gown.

Desire surged in his blood as she smiled at him. Such a warm and open smile. So different from the calculated simpering he'd grown used to.

"Your mom is staring at us." Tessa leaned in.

He could smell the scent of her. Rich and sweet, like honeyed baklava. "Do you think she's upset you're spending so much time dancing with your assistant?" Concern troubled her green eyes.

"No." He leaned in and couldn't resist planting a soft kiss on her ear. "Perhaps she's transfixed by your ravishing beauty."

Tessa blinked.

"Have I embarrassed you?" he said softly.

"Yes." She flashed a glance at him. "I was taught to beware flatterers."

"Wise advice. But many women would be upset if no one stared at them."

Faris, for example. She lived for the spotlight. He kept hoping its bright light would attract a suitor she couldn't resist, so she'd stop trying to sink her manicured talons into him.

His mother had assured him that Faris was "waiting for him."

That was going to be a long wait.

"What are you smiling at?" Tessa smiled, too. He eased closer. Her high heels made her almost his height, and they danced pressed to each other from cheek to hip. Their feet barely moved, though other guests swirled around them to the music.

His blood pulsed in time with the drumbeat. He had to work hard to keep his hands from creeping down to enjoy the curve of her pert bottom.

Her back called to his fingertips, bare in her low-cut dress.

Tessa's cool fingers crept over his shirt collar and roamed into his hair.

He pulled her closer still. Her hips swayed against his,

rhythmic, hypnotic. When he glanced down, her eyes had closed. Her lovely face shone with a rapt expression.

A thick sensation built inside Sebastian's chest. A thicker one started to pound between his legs.

She'd forgotten everyone else in the room. Given herself to the music, their dance.

To him.

Sebastian laid a soft kiss on her neck and she writhed against him.

Her sensual movements surprised him.

Had she forgotten they were surrounded by a thousand people?

Decades of stern training kept him on high alert at all times. Ready to represent the nation of Caspia in everything he did.

But now even he was beginning to lose his firm grip on protocol and etiquette.

Tessa's fingers wound around his neck, pulling his face to hers.

Then their lips met in a cool, fresh kiss.

She tasted like mint. Sharp, spicy and bracing.

Her cool tongue challenged his to a duel, and he couldn't help but spar and parry with it, claiming her mouth in a kiss that deepened with each beat of the music.

The beaded fabric of her dress stirred his senses as he ran his hands over her curves, imagining the feel of the smooth skin beneath.

Hard inside his tailored pants, he suppressed a groan as her soft, wet tongue licked his lips.

He wanted her.

Now.

"Tessa." He growled the word more than spoke it. His

blood had departed his brain for more primal regions of his body.

She didn't respond except to clutch him closer.

Her fingers now ran over his suit jacket, plucking at the stiff fabric.

He fought the urge to peel it off.

"Tessa." He breathed it, trying to arch away from her, his arousal so intense it hurt.

"Sebastian," she rasped, her body pressed to his, still swaying and swinging to the music.

Then she gasped and sprang back.

She staggered back a few feet, crashing into an older couple. The gray-haired old fellow was almost bent double under the weight of his ceremonial medals and he pitched to one side.

"Oh, goodness." She grabbed his arm and righted him. "I'm so sorry!" She glanced at Sebastian, her eyes wide.

She patted her hair, as if it was wild and windblown. A pink flush spread over her cheeks, contrasting prettily with the cool green of her dress.

Sebastian had never seen a more enticing vision.

"Let's go somewhere quiet," he told her.

Her eyes widened. "But we can't. *You* can't." She glanced out at the crowd of dancers swirling around them.

"Oh, yes, I can." Resolve, and painful longing, thickened his voice.

"But it's your family's party. Your parents will be upset if you... They'll think I'm some kind of..." Her blush deepened.

"I don't care what they think. You'd better come with me now, or I'll have the palace guards arrest you and bring you to me."

He saw his own excitement reflected right back at him in sparkling green.

"Gee. I've never been arrested by palace guards before. I might like it."

"Don't tempt me."

"I think I already did."

Her bright gaze dropped to the unseemly bulge beneath his pants.

His erection throbbed.

"If you don't come with me right now, you're in danger of high treason."

Her mouth formed a provocative O.

"It's a capital offense."

She tilted her head and narrowed her bright eyes. "Have a lot of women sacrificed their lives defending their virtue?"

"Not a single one."

His eyes roamed hungrily over the glittering green of her dress, shimmering under the lights like a mermaid's lithe tail.

He couldn't wait. He reached out and grabbed her arm. Her skin felt hot against his palm. The ache in his groin intensified as he pulled her close and wrapped his arm around her waist.

She stiffened, but he didn't loosen his grip. There was no way he'd let her get away now.

He knew she wanted him every bit as much as he wanted her.

Eight

"Where on earth is Sebastian going with that young woman?" Rania, Queen of Caspia, leaned toward her husband. Even her favorite Vivaldi made her head ache tonight.

"I can't say, dear."

"You may not want to say, but I think we both have a pretty good idea. When is that boy going to grow up?"

"Sebastian is thirty-four years old. I think most people would say he is grown up."

Ugh! Her husband could be so obtuse. He simply stood there, staring out over the crowds. All their friends and the crowned heads of every remaining monarchy in Europe gathered under this roof tonight.

While their only son crept off to go get naked with…a servant.

She shivered.

"She's his assistant, for God's sake!"

"Lovely girl."

Her husband's silver hair still curled elegantly around his majestic head. He had the same proud profile and easy good humor that had driven her half-wild as an impressionable girl.

These days he sometimes drove her completely mad.

"Have you forgotten that our son is the future king of Caspia?"

"I am aware of that."

"He should be courting women of his own stature. Girls of noble blood."

"I'm sure Sebastian will choose an excellent wife."

"Sure, are you? What makes you so sure? Lately I don't feel sure of anything."

She fanned herself with a linen cocktail napkin. Another of those awful hot flashes, come to remind her of her own mortality and that the future lay with the next generation.

Which Sebastian might be creating right now with his own office assistant.

She fanned harder.

Her husband turned to her.

Oh, dear. His *stern* look.

"Rania, darling. Sebastian is high-spirited, yes. But he is Caspian to the core. He loves our country and its people with all his soul. He'll rise to the task of devoting his life to them as their king. Why shouldn't he have some fun before he assumes the weighty mantle of responsibility?"

"Oh. Did you miss out on all that fun by marrying me too young?"

"Rania." He pressed a soft kiss behind her ear.

Her knees still buckled slightly when he did that. Her heart softened toward her warm and trusting husband.

"Sweetheart, I'm just worried, that's all. Wouldn't it be better for everyone if he was safely settled down with a nice girl like Faris?"

"Faris is a lot of things. Nice isn't one of them."

Her husband stared out again at the crowds, his expression rigid.

"Darling, Faris is the daughter of your oldest friend. What on earth would Deon say if he heard you?"

"I don't intend for him to hear me, but I don't intend to encourage my son to be a martyr to Faris Maridis, either."

"But they've known each other almost since birth. After our own, her family is the most prominent and oldest in Caspia. She's beautiful. Surely you'll admit that?"

"Yes. No question. She is beautiful. And I pity the poor sod who gets dazzled into marrying her."

"But what if Sebastian does choose someone like his own secretary? Stubborn as he is, he's quite capable of it." She fanned herself again, feeling breathless and faint. "Not only is she American, she's not even from money. Sebastian admitted it himself."

Her husband raised an eyebrow. "You asked him?"

"Well, yes. Why not?"

Her husband burst into a guffaw of laughter.

Rania frowned. Very briefly. Then she reassumed her habitual public expression of beatific contentment.

It wasn't easy being queen.

The French champagne tasted bitter and foul to Faris.

Right in front of everyone!

Pawing at each other like teenagers. That girl with her head thrown back, eyes closed, swaying in his arms.

Disgusting.

And Sebastian grappling her like a rugby opponent. Without a thought for all their friends and family in attendance.

Anger and humiliation clawed at her gut.

She'd laughed off his dalliances with starlets and socialites. Those fluffy girls were no match for Sebastian Stone. She was invariably gratified when he appeared in the papers with a different girl-of-the-moment the following week.

She really shouldn't concern herself over this scrawny American girl who filed his papers for a living.

Faris adjusted her beautiful midnight-colored dress over her creamy décolletage.

Tessa Banks was a nobody. A member of staff.

So why had Sebastian clung to her as though she held the secret to eternal life?

He'd stared at her. Stroked her.

Kissed her.

She'd never seen that look of distracted preoccupation on his face before.

Faris touched her hair to make sure her chignon was still perfect. You never knew when someone would snap a picture.

Sebastian was *hers*.

They'd both known that since birth. Their mothers had joked about their future marriage from the time they fought over rattles on a blanket spread in the palace gardens.

It was fate.

Destiny.

She would one day be Queen Faris of Caspia.

She didn't mind waiting. She'd waited thirty-four years, for crying out loud! Lucky thing she didn't look a day over twenty-five. But people were starting to talk. It was time for the marriage to happen.

She was determined to extract a proposal from him this year.

By any means necessary.

The sound of the party faded as Sebastian led Tessa down a long corridor. Her heels clacked on the stone floor as she tried to keep up with his swift steps.

"In here." He tugged her into a darkened room and closed the door. Tessa tried to catch her breath. She couldn't see a thing. Electricity crackled in the air between her and Sebastian, heightened by their lightning escape from the party.

A light bloomed under Sebastian's hand. An oil lamp, set into a recess in the wall.

"We don't use electric light in here. Too many precious items that might fade."

"Where are we?" She still couldn't see much in the pulsing gloom of the lamp. A sultry scent, like sandalwood, hung faint in the air.

"This is the oldest part of the palace. The walls here are six-feet thick. No one will hear us."

Desire thickened his voice.

Tessa's face heated and her breasts tingled beneath her dress.

He lit another oil lamp, illuminating a low seating area in a corner of the room. Gold thread shone in the lush fabrics and brocade dangled from thick pillows.

Sebastian took her hand, his skin hot on hers. "Are you tired from dancing?" He stroked her cheek with his thumb.

"Not at all." Excitement hummed in her blood. Her voice sounded breathless. "You?"

He answered her with a hot, hard kiss that stole the last

of her senses. His hands roamed over her dress, over her breasts, her backside, her thighs, with rough and lusty movements quite unlike his restraint at the party.

His eyes were so dark they appeared black, bottomless and brimming with desire.

For a moment she thought he might rip off her couture dress in one swift movement. But he turned her gently, his hands at her waist. He undid the hooks and eyes along the back of her dress with skilled fingers. Even if the expense meant nothing to him, Sebastian appreciated the artistry and hard work that went into designer originals. The heavy, beaded fabric slid over her like a lover's caress.

"You were beautiful in the dress, but without it…" He exhaled softly.

His fingers sparked trails of shimmering excitement. He unhooked her bra and carefully removed it. A slight breeze through a high window stung her nipples to tight awareness.

She tried not to wobble as he layered kisses along her spine. Kneeling behind her, he tugged her skimpy silk panties down over her legs, until she wore nothing but her strappy high heels.

He stood and she turned to face him. The look on his face transfixed her. Raw lust, yes, but something deeper and more powerful shone in his eyes and hardened his strong features.

Desire echoed through her like a crack of thunder. He'd shed his jacket and she'd been reaching up to unbutton his shirt, but suddenly her hands fell lower, and they both struggled with the fly of his pants, shoved them down and rolled on the condom.

He entered her slowly, cupping her buttocks as she pressed the length of her body against his. Aroused almost to boiling point, she gripped him as he thrust his hard length into her.

Against her back, the cool stone of an ancient column felt heavenly. It held her upright as Sebastian devoured her mouth and drove into her body with forceful thrusts.

The pent-up taut desire that had built like a fire while they danced could no longer be contained. Tremors rippled between them as their bellies clashed. Sebastian's rough kisses only strengthened her agonizing craving to draw him closer. To become one, even for a moment.

The mere touch of his lips unleashed a starburst of bright light and color in front of her eyes. The teasing scratch of his nails set her skin shivering and tingling.

She bucked against him, taking him deeper, clawing at the fabric of his shirt.

Sebastian thrust harder, taking her further on the journey out of her body and mind and into an alternate dimension of fierce, pounding desire that made her blood thunder in her veins.

The world dissolved—along with all barriers between them—as they exploded into orgasm. The rush was so intense that Tessa lost consciousness for a split second before she crashed back to life in Sebastian's strong arms.

Bittersweet relief rang through her as the tension slipped from her body and she held on to her lover for dear life.

Sebastian released a groan in her ear. His shirt was bunched up over the thick muscles of his chest, forgotten in their urgency. Tessa's arms were fast under it, wrapped around his hot, perspiring skin.

His heady male scent stole over her senses, making her want to bury her face in his neck and drink him in.

"Much better," he murmured, holding her tight.

She wanted to laugh, but she knew exactly how he felt. "Me, too." Still, her legs were shaking. "Maybe we should sit down before we fall down."

"Good idea." He eased out of her carefully and she shivered, already craving him inside her again.

Worse yet, he disappeared into the shadows, leaving her naked against the cool stone pillar.

He returned with a long sweep of silk fabric. "Lift your arms."

She obeyed. He wrapped the material, purple with a gold border, around her with practiced movements, then secured it at her shoulder with a gold pin. The fine silk fell to the floor, billowing slightly in the breeze.

"I feel like I've stepped into a myth."

"Maybe you have." His deep voice rippled through the air like smoke.

She gasped as Sebastian swept her right off her spike-heeled feet and into his arms. He marched across the room and laid her gently on soft cushions in the sitting area.

A bowl of fragrant oil smoldered over a tiny candle, filling the room with its seductive scent.

"Champagne?"

Sebastian had stripped off his crumpled shirt and his bronzed torso gleamed in the scant light.

"Um, sure."

He moved to a wall behind her, and drew out a bottle.

"What is this room used for?" She still couldn't make out much in the dark.

"It's the antechamber behind the throne room. Guests are sometimes entertained here during official functions."

"Ah. That explains the champagne." She took the offered glass, bubbles sparkling in the warm glow from the candle. "And you keep silk robes on hand in case anyone spills Bollinger on their clothes?"

Sebastian smiled slowly. "The robe you're wearing is from our national collection. It was created by royal weavers who once did nothing but create cloth for the family."

"Oh, goodness." Tessa's skin shrank from the priceless history draped over it. "I'm not sure I should be wearing it. I'm kind of sweaty."

Sebastian shrugged. "What's the use of keeping something that cannot be worn? The weavers put their heart and skill into creating the finest fabrics known to mankind. I'm sure they'd rather their efforts caress a beautiful woman glowing with the heat of passion, than sit in a trunk waiting for moths to find them."

Glowing. Okay, that worked. "The silk is as soft as fleece. Was it made recently?"

Sebastian made a wry expression. "No, I'm afraid royal weavers went the way of the royal soothsayers. The events of the twentieth century encroached on Caspia as they did every corner of Europe. It's a miracle that we still have our treasures. The crown jewels are kept locked in the vault here, too. Would you like to see them?"

Tessa's eyebrows shot up. "Sure, I'd love to." She started to get up.

"Wait here. I'll bring them to you."

The mysterious gleam in his eye made her stomach flutter. Or was that an aftershock from her orgasm? She sipped her champagne and fanned herself, which made the incense flame flicker.

Sebastian returned with a large box of dark wood, intricately carved with figures. His thick arms strained under its weight.

"Goodness, what's in there? Gold bricks?"

He chuckled and studied her face, her neck.

She heated under his regard.

He lifted the lid, reached into the box and plucked out something shiny. "This one."

Something sparkled in the dim light, but she couldn't make out details.

Sebastian reached over her shoulders and laid cool, heavy metal on her collarbones. He fastened it behind her neck.

"Beautiful."

"It's a necklace?" She touched it with her fingers. The metal was heavily ornamented, encrusted with jewels. Carnelian maybe? It was hard to tell in the darkness. "What are these?"

"Rubies."

She sucked in a breath. "And the necklace is gold?"

"Twenty-four karat."

"Isn't pure gold very soft?"

"Yes, that's why it must be saved for special occasions." He looked right into her eyes. "Like tonight."

That fluttering sensation again.

Sebastian pulled out another gem-encrusted treasure. "Hold out your right wrist."

He fastened the linked bracelet, heavy as a manacle and almost as tight, around her wrist. "You're slim, like the ancient people. It fits you perfectly." He caressed her wrist with his thumb.

"How old are these pieces?"

"They date back at least to the time of the Byzantine Empire, but they may be centuries, even millennia older. Caspia was sacked in 550 A.D. during the reign of Justinian. The library was burned and all records destroyed. Our history up to that point is as much legend as fact."

He plucked out a slim ring of gold, like a headband. He turned it so the single gem was at the front, then settled it on her forehead.

Like a crown.

Tessa felt her face heat. As much from Sebastian's serious expression as from the weird situation.

Never in her wildest dreams had she imagined she'd wind up sitting in the Caspian Palace, dressed as a royal princess. Suddenly she felt like a chimp decked out for a tea party.

"Why so jumpy?"

"It's just weird, that's all. I don't feel right in these things."

Sebastian took her hand and pulled her gently to her feet. "Nonsense." He took a couple of steps back. She stood there, swaying in her heels, as his eyes roamed over her, searing her flesh right through the thin silk. "These jewels are flattered by your beauty." His voice rumbled, echoing slightly off the stone walls. "As if they were made for you."

Sebastian couldn't take his eyes off her.

His golden goddess, tall and regal, her striking features chiseled by the chiaroscuro of candlelight. The draping silk displayed her magnificent body to perfection and the heavy majesty of the gold pieces enhanced her natural proud stance.

He couldn't think. Could barely breathe.

"It's just me. Tessa." Her green eyes were wary.

"I know. That's why I can't stop staring."

"It must be kind of bizarre seeing your royal jewels on a regular person. I'd better take them off."

"No!" The word flew out. "I love to see you in them. Partly because you are 'a regular person' as you call it. I love that about you. You're not jaded and bored with the pleasures of life, like so many women I meet."

"I guess that's because I haven't had the opportunity to burn out yet. A few more grand balls, a hundred more boat trips in the harbor, a thousand gallops across the countryside and I might be yawning behind my champagne glass, too." Her eyes sparkled.

"Never."

"How do you know?"

"I'm a good judge of character."

She lifted her chin. "I did get bored with being your assistant."

He couldn't help smiling. "I don't blame you. It was a boring job."

"I'm afraid I'm better at riding than at typing correspondence."

"Most emphatically."

Her eyes widened.

"I didn't mean that your correspondence is lacking," he turned to add. "Just that you're being wasted on it. You're meant for so much more than sitting at a desk, talking on the phone."

"Like what?" She crossed her arms over her chest, the provocative and unladylike gesture a sharp and delicious contrast with the traditional attire.

He loved it.

You are meant to be my queen.

His brain threw out the words. He blinked, swallowed and cleared his throat. "Let's sleep in my bed," he rasped.

Her eyes widened.

"There's a secret passage. No one will see us." He knew Tessa would prefer to keep it a secret and he wanted to preserve her modesty.

He scooped up the box. "We'll take these with us. I think I need to see them all on you."

She laughed. "I won't argue. A girl doesn't get dressed up in ancient treasures every day."

He gathered their clothes, and with his arm around her waist, he led her through the low, arched doorway in the thick walls, and along the dark, cold passage that led from the old palace to the relatively modern fourteenth-century wing.

On the dark silk sheets of his bed, he dressed her in deep blue lapis, the gold-flecked stone mystical in the candlelight against her golden skin.

Then emeralds. The heavy collar circled her slender neck and brought out the vivid green of her eyes.

Magic.

The familiar environment of his bedroom—the room he had slept in since birth and which he would one day share with his wife—seemed transformed by her presence.

True, he had invited girls to try on the royal collection before. This particular seduction technique was surefire. He'd recommend it to anyone with a priceless collection of ancient treasures and a beautiful but hesitant woman.

Right now, he was the one being seduced. Not by the sight of hammered gold or precious jewels, but by the splendid woman wearing them.

"You're spoiling me, Sebastian. What if I wake up tomorrow and just don't feel like myself without emeralds on?"

"There's an easy cure for that. Emeralds."

"Being a prince definitely makes you lose touch with reality."

"I'm in touch with reality," he protested. Mostly he wanted to touch her breasts, high and enticing. Or her thighs, sleek, long and gleaming in the warm light.

"There won't be any emeralds in my life once I go home."

He frowned. Go home? Why on earth was she thinking about that now? The prospect wrenched at his gut.

"There will always be emeralds in your life," he growled. "Your eyes."

Her sweet laughter tickled his ears. "You're sweeping me off my feet and it's not a nice thing to do. I have a regular life to go back to. I think Caspia has ruined me for everywhere else."

"You're falling in love with our country?"

She startled a little when he said the *L* word.

Truth be told, he did, too.

She recovered quickly. "How could I not? Everything about it is perfect. The sea, the sky, the mountains, the lovely people."

"The dust, the flies, roaming goats, the smell of raw fish." He narrowed his eyes and tried not to smile.

Her eyes shone. "Exactly. They're all perfect."

His chest tightened as a rush of feeling flowed through him. He did love everything about his country. Even the things others might criticize. Now Tessa felt the same?

Perfect.

She'd better not be thinking about going back to Phil or Paul or whatever his name was. Throwing her life away in a gamble for some elusive happy-ever-after.

He'd cure her of him.

By the time he was done with her tonight, she wouldn't be able to think about anyone. She'd be too exhausted, satiated and suffused with pleasure to remember her own name.

He'd make sure of it.

Desire shivered through him. He wanted her naked again, with nothing between them. The jewels ornamented her beauty, but didn't enhance it.

Tessa was most beautiful as simply herself.

He unhooked the heavy emerald necklace and pressed a warm kiss to her lips.

Her tongue sneaked into his mouth as she kissed him back with passion. Forgotten, the strings of green gems slid between her lush, high breasts and got lost somewhere down in the sheets.

Sebastian got lost somewhere in her lips, in the soft embrace of her arms and the rich sweet scent of her.

When he made love to her again, he didn't think about charming her or cajoling her or trying to win her over.

He couldn't think about anything. His heart was too full with emotions he couldn't name.

His heart?

His friends teased him for being heartless, but Sebastian always laughed it off. He wasn't heartless. In fact, he was very affectionate and caring.

Just on a short-term basis.

But tonight...

Tessa's head lay on the pillow next to him, her golden lashes lowered in sweet sleep, her hair flung back from her lovely face.

He drew in a long, sharp breath, which didn't ease the strange fullness in his chest.

He had a heart, all right. And he was in serious danger of losing it.

Nine

Tessa didn't show up at breakfast.

Not to worry, Sebastian told himself. She was a big girl and he wasn't her shadow.

Sebastian sat at the table and helped himself to some eggs. His dad was immersed in the London *Times* and his mom was already gabbing on the phone about some charity luncheon.

He yawned and reached for the silver tray with his mail. He tried to forget the groaning stack of unread correspondence in his New York apartment. A couple of party invitations. A postcard from his pal Ravi, trekking in Nepal. He slit open a slim ivory envelope with his silver opener.

He saw black letters, printed so neatly a machine could have done it.

You are the future King of Caspia.
Your children will rule Caspia one day.
Do not insult our nation and take a foreign bride.
Especially one who is of low birth.

There was a long gap on the paper.
Then the words.

Like Tessa Banks.

Sebastian's empty stomach growled, as much with rage as hunger. Who *dared* to insult Tessa in this way?

He lifted the coffeepot from its open-flame burner and placed the crumpled sheet directly on the flames. It withered into a leaf, then turned to ash.

His mother looked up. "What on earth are you doing, dear?"

"Destroying trash."

"You could have asked Theo for a wastepaper basket."

"Yes." He ripped off a hunk of fresh bread. He was used to petty jealousies and trumped-up scandals. Gossipmongers looking for drama.

They came with the territory of monarchy.

Already the note drifted from his mind like the burned-out embers.

In the spacious palace offices, Tessa spread her notes and contact information out on an antique desk. She planned to call all the meeting attendees to confirm their arrival times and remind them what was expected of them

She'd even dressed in a smart beige pantsuit. She was here on business, and intended to remind people of that fact. Lately she'd noticed the staff giving her sideways looks in the hallways. No doubt they wondered what she was up to, gallivanting all over Caspia with their prince when she was here to arrange a meeting and organize some files.

Whatever they were thinking, she'd prove them wrong.

Well, not *wrong,* exactly. It was a bit late for that.

She pushed her hair out of her eyes and blew out a breath.

She'd succumbed to Sebastian's charms like so many other women before her.

She probably never stood a chance. Everything about Sebastian was intoxicating. His energy and spirit, his warmth and passion, his kindness and—

Hello, you have a job to do.

Tessa flipped through the numbers in her PDA and was about to dial the first.

Then she hesitated. She suddenly remembered the way Sebastian had looked at her last night, as she sat on his magnificent bed, decked out in his country's royal splendor.

The memory took her breath away. His eyes, dark and wide and so full of…love.

Impossible?

Suddenly hot, she lifted her hair off her neck. It was hard to think. Thoughts of Sebastian consumed her mind and tormented her body.

She couldn't forget his rough yet gentle hands on her body, his rousing kisses, or the lovemaking that left her gasping and shivering with ecstasy.

Then there were his intimate conversation, his genial smiles and encouraging caresses.

Of course, he was warm and enthusiastic with everyone. Sebastian never met a person, or an animal, he didn't like. She'd even seen him give a friendly and encouraging pat to an olive tree.

She couldn't help smiling as her chest filled with affection for him.

They'd worked together for nearly five years and their relationship had always been professional. Cordial. Polite.

Suddenly it was so different.

He'd danced with her in front of hundreds of guests at the ball. Held her and kissed her as if she was his…girlfriend. Was she totally delusional in imagining it as a possibility?

Her PDA screen had gone blank. *Hey, you're here to work.* She snapped herself to attention and punched the button to make the first call. It would be embarrassing if no one showed up for the meeting.

Still, she wondered if Sebastian was already looking for her. Maybe even heading toward her right now.

Her fingers and toes tingled with delicious anticipation.

Once the first round of phone calls was made, the sun was high in the sky. She decided to step out onto the terrace outside the offices and enjoy the view of the harbor and some heliotheraphy while she typed the agenda from her notes.

She stepped over the threshold, put her laptop on a carved, stone table and stretched.

Then she noticed someone watching her.

A tall, slim woman. Standing on the far side of the long terrace, in the opposite direction from the harbor.

"Ms. Banks." The woman's voice rang out across the stone tiles.

"Hello?" Tessa squinted in the sun. It wasn't the queen, but she looked vaguely familiar.

Faris. The woman from last night with the blue dress and the snotty remarks. What was she doing here?

Faris marched toward her, heels clicking on the stone tiles. A long white dress draped over her slender yet voluptuous body.

"I imagine you're busy arranging all the details of your little meeting."

Tessa's back stiffened. "It's a pretty big meeting. Thirty principals."

Faris waved an elegant hand. A tinkly laugh grated on Tessa's ears. "How tiresome to put it all together. I do admire you working girls. I'd never be able to keep up a fake smile while wading through all that drudgery."

"Hardly drudgery here on this lovely terrace. I couldn't be happier." Tessa forced a bright smile. Her hand itched to slap Faris's expertly made-up cheek, but she managed to resist.

"It must be marvelous to be content with so little. But I suppose you get used to it." Faris glanced out at the horizon, as if deep in philosophical contemplation. "I imagine the difficult part will be going back to the rat race once you've become used to living in a palace."

"I suspect I'll manage." Tessa arranged her papers on the table. She tried not to think about how hard it really would be to return to the dreary world of subway platforms and electric bills.

There wasn't going to be any liberating move to California now. By sleeping with Sebastian she'd slammed the door on that possible future.

Unease tightened her muscles, along with guilt that she'd cheated on Patrick and fear of what lay ahead of her now. She wasn't really foolish enough to think that she had a future with Sebastian.

Was she?

"Sebastian's such a charmer, isn't he?" Faris stood over her, casting a long shadow across Tessa's notes. "Let me guess. He gave you his famous 'royal treatment.'"

Tessa frowned. "Sebastian has been very gracious."

Faris tilted her head. "Which did he choose first? The gold diadem or the emerald necklace?" A smile played about her perfectly shaped mouth.

Tessa's own mouth dropped open.

"Oh, come on. Just between us girls. Those rubies are heavy, aren't they?"

"I—I don't know what you're talking about." She swallowed hard.

Faris narrowed her dark eyes. "Did you think you were special?" She pouted. "Oh. Sebastian can be quite wicked. Don't take it personally, though. He doesn't mean to break your heart, he just can't help it."

Her laugh rattled in the air. "And you shouldn't feel bad, either. Half the women of Europe have worn those jewels with stars in their eyes, myself included."

Tessa was seeing stars in front of her eyes right now. Her desire to slap Faris was morphing into a desire to get face-to-face with Sebastian and—

She sucked in a deep breath. "I hate to be so…bourgeois, but I'm afraid I have work to do."

Faris smiled. "Of course you do. I just thought I should warn you. That's all. As a *friend*."

The final word dripped with malice.

Tessa's good cheer plummeted with each farewell click of Faris's sharp heels.

She sagged into the cushioned wrought iron chair. The bright sun and the glare of white buildings and blue sea hurt her eyes.

How naive could she be?

Did she really think Sebastian dressed her up like a queen because he wanted to make her *his* queen?

It was a little fun foreplay for him.

A practiced seduction technique.

Not that he needed to seduce her. She'd been ready to rip his clothes off on the dance floor.

Besides, they'd already made love—no, scratch that, they'd had sex—before he started weighing her down with jewels.

She drew in a ragged breath. She had nothing to be ashamed of. She hadn't begged to get decked out like a Homerian goddess. It was all his idea.

And he had enjoyed it.

Even now her heart swelled as she remembered the caress of his dark eyes. Of his big, gentle hands.

Her PDA vibrated and she picked it up.

The number on the screen made her heart thud.

She inhaled and composed herself. "Hi, Sebastian. How are you?"

"That depends on how you are." His low, seductive voice tickled her ear.

"I'm fine."

"Theo told me you had breakfast early so you could get to work."

"Yes. I had to call the meeting attendees. Make sure they're coming." She could barely get the words out. "I'm about to type the agenda."

"Can you fit me into your agenda today?" His tone

was warm and flirtatious. She couldn't help a stirring of excitement in her chest.

Then the image of Faris, mocking her about the jewels, cooled her blood. "You're the boss."

"Oh, yeah. I forgot about that. Want to go for a ride?"

"I can't. I haven't even started the agenda yet and the meeting is tomorrow. Let me get it typed up so you can look at it. This afternoon I'll print and collate the copies."

"I'm sure someone else could do all that."

"It's my job."

"Magna misses you."

"Who?"

"Your horse. She told me this morning."

"Oh, stop." She couldn't resist chuckling. "She's probably plotting her revenge."

"I'm plotting my revenge. I can't believe you beat me to the top of the crag last time. I've got a reputation to defend."

Tessa's blood heated with the thought of racing up the mountainside on the athletic and bighearted mare.

The prospect of another carefree, exhilarating day with Sebastian.

But it wouldn't be the same. Not now that she knew the magical night they'd shared had been a standard offering from his well-worn repertoire.

Her heart clenched. "I wish I could, but there's so little time left that I need to focus and get this done. I've goofed off enough already."

"It doesn't count as goofing off when it's on the boss's orders."

He sounded so cheerful. He obviously thought he had her thoroughly under his spell.

Which was true, until a few minutes ago.

She actually owed a debt of gratitude to the mean-spirited Faris.

"I should command you to cease and desist all tiresome administrative activities."

"I'm not in the mood to be commanded."

"I might be."

Oh, why could she picture his mischievous grin so clearly? Her chest hurt with trying to fight off emotion.

"Seriously, I *want* to get this done." At least then she would have actually accomplished something here in Caspia other than being Sebastian's Playmate-of-the-Week.

"Okay, okay. But don't miss lunch or I'll have the royal guard hunt you down. One o'clock in the dining room."

"Sure." She hung up.

She could make it through another lunch. Another dinner even. She could smile and be polite and hold her chin up.

The meeting was tomorrow and after that she could begin the heartbreaking process of leaving behind the most wonderful days of her life.

Of trying to forget Sebastian.

"Tessa!" Sebastian rose to greet her as she entered the dining room on trembling legs. She hadn't seen Sebastian's parents—aka the king and queen—since her embarrassing display at the ball the previous night.

"Good afternoon," she said with what she hoped was an obsequious nod.

"Come sit here next to Mama." Sebastian indicated an empty chair. His mother looked every bit as surprised and not-delighted as Tessa. What was he trying to pull?

She did like the way he still called his mother "Mama." It was kind of cute.

For a womanizing jerk.

Sebastian held out the chair next to his mother for Tessa then returned to his seat on the other side of her. His father sat farther down the table, perusing a newspaper folded open to the crossword puzzle.

The prickly and poised Queen of Caspia surveyed Tessa down the length of her elegant nose. "How are preparations for the meeting coming?"

Tessa opened her mouth to reply, but Sebastian cut her off.

"She doesn't want to talk about that boring stuff. Didn't she look radiant at the dance last night?"

His dark eyes shone with the same admiration she dimly remembered from— Oh, my gosh. It was only this morning he'd layered soft, wet kisses over her neck and breasts.

"Yes. That was a pretty dress, dear. From one of your new boutiques?" She managed her entire response without glancing at Tessa.

Sebastian shot Tessa a warm smile. He didn't seem to notice she wasn't glowing back. A young man in a white uniform served her bread and salads, and she tried to eat a bite or two. But it was hard.

Last night had been so magical. So special and so perfect.

And now here was Sebastian right in front of her. Brawny arms revealed by the rolled-up sleeves of his white linen shirt, and his sun-bronzed face creased in a cheery grin.

He was exactly the same person he'd been yesterday. The easygoing royal playboy who dated a different girl every week.

It was she who had changed.

Her throat dried as she realized the full extent of the problem.

She'd fallen in love with him.

"…haven't forgotten the Sons of the Garter benefit tonight, have you?" Sebastian's mother leaned forward.

Sebastian frowned. "Oh, that again? I thought I just survived the last one."

"These men are our nation's heroes. Some of them fought in World War II."

"I think *all* of them fought in World War II. There can't be a man under eighty in the Order of the Garter."

"All the more reason to pay your respects and celebrate their achievements. It's part of your royal duty."

She underscored the last two words with a slight growl that made Tessa jump in her chair.

"I know, and I do appreciate their sacrifices." Sebastian looked at Tessa and leaned forward. "These men have some amazing stories to tell. Wait till you hear Leo Kahn talk about the time he—"

"Tessa won't be there." The queen's lips were so tight the words barely came out. "The event is for gentlemen only."

Sebastian shot an apologetic glance at Tessa. She resisted the urge to sag in her chair with relief. She couldn't imagine spending another night at his side, pretending to be cheerful and gregarious when her heart was crushed and bleeding inside her.

"Besides, I imagine Tessa will be busy with preparations for the meeting. It's not fair to divert members of staff from their duties for your own entertainment."

She shot a piercing glance at Tessa and then punctuated it with an icy smile that froze Tessa's already shrunken stomach.

Sebastian waved a dismissive hand. "Tessa's never been to Caspia before. She represents our country every day in the business we do. It's essential that she become familiar with our nation."

The queen stabbed a piece of tomato, then glared at Sebastian with narrowed eyes. "There's such a thing as being *too* familiar."

"Too familiar?" The king's gruff voice chimed in. "Impossible. The whole world should know our nation like an intimate friend." His twinkly smile eased the tension in Tessa's gut. "Which aspects of our country have you enjoyed so far, my dear?"

Your son.

Tessa swallowed hard. "Sebastian was kind enough to take me for a ride in the mountains. I can't say I've ever had a more wonderful experience in my life." Her voice cracked a bit on the last sentence, and she looked down at her plate.

"Ah, the mountains. Said like a true Caspian. People praise our calm water and our classical buildings, but a Caspian knows the mountains are the bones of our country and our source of strength. They've protected us from invasion for hundreds of years. I like nothing better than a ride in the mountains, myself." The king leaned toward her, a look of genuine warmth on his face.

Tessa shrank back. He wouldn't be so friendly if he knew what she'd been doing with his only son last night. If he knew that she, Tessa Banks, secretary—nobody—

had entertained mad and delusional thoughts that Sebastian might actually care for her.

That right now she was rendered speechless by unfamiliar and painful feelings for him.

"Tessa—" the queen's voice cut into her thoughts "—are all the attendees for the meeting confirmed?"

She cleared her throat and tried to sound calm. "All except one. Pierre de Rochefauld of Château D'Arc winery has been hard to reach."

"Filthy stuff, anyway." The queen spoke to Sebastian. "Loaded with sulfites. Their Bordeaux gave me a frightful migraine last time I drank it."

"Everything gives you a migraine lately, Mama. You should stick to our Caspian grappa." Sebastian took her hand and squeezed it. Tessa was surprised to see the Queen of Mean pat her son's face affectionately.

Maybe she wasn't made entirely of Caspian marble.

Queen Rania's steely gaze returned to spear Tessa. "So all is ready for the meeting?"

"Not quite. I still need to make copies of the agenda, and I have some research to do in the files."

"We mustn't keep you." The queen raised her brows as she attacked another slice of tomato.

"You're right. I must get back to work." Tessa sprang from her chair, glad of the chance to escape.

"I'll come with you." Sebastian was up and halfway around the table before he'd finished speaking.

"Sebastian! You promised you'd take me to the new Ferragamo boutique this afternoon."

Sebastian leaned over his mother and kissed her on the cheek. "Mama, you've been to every Ferragamo boutique in the world. I'm sure you can handle it by yourself."

The queen pouted and shot a glance at her husband. Tessa scurried from the room, heart pounding, with Sebastian behind her like a shadow.

"Don't mind Mama. She's not always such an old battle-ax," he whispered, as they hurried along an empty corridor. "She's going through the change of life and it's making her cranky."

Tessa didn't think hormones were involved. More likely Queen Rania felt it beneath her dignity to eat lunch with her son's whore-of-the-moment.

But Sebastian's apologetic expression, combined with the intimate family confession, tugged at something inside her.

Then she remembered Faris's words: *He doesn't mean to break your heart. He just can't help it.*

And apparently she just couldn't help having her heart broken. How could she not fall for Sebastian? She'd been carrying a secret torch for him for years. Now that she'd gotten to know him even better, now that they'd shared joyful adventures and breathtaking intimacies… It should be no surprise she was done for.

She hurried along the corridor. "You should take your mom shopping. I have a lot to do."

"I'll help you with your work." His hand on her arm made her start. She pulled back carefully, ignoring the heat left by his palm.

"There's nothing at all challenging to it. I just need to locate some missing audits. Things that didn't make it to New York for whatever reason. We never received the files on Château D'Arc."

"And now you can't get in touch with the company principal?"

"No. He's the owner, too. He inherited the wine business along with the family estate. I've been meaning to follow up more aggressively, but I haven't had time." She shot him an accusatory look.

"Hmm. I'll call him from the offices."

"That might be a good idea, actually. His assistant keeps making strange excuses. I get a weird feeling he's actually there when I call. He'd come to the phone for you."

"Royalty has its privileges." Sebastian winked.

Tessa smiled, then it withered on her lips as she remembered all the privileges he'd taken with her last night. It probably didn't even cross his mind that a night like that could haunt her forever.

He'd probably already started to forget it. He'd think no more of her than Senator Kendrick would have if she'd let him kiss her because he was a senator. Wealthy and powerful men had no need to consider the feelings of others.

By next week, Sebastian would be flirting and laughing with someone else.

"What's the matter?"

"Nothing." Her breathing had become audible. The thought of Sebastian with another woman was a knife to her gut.

Which was ridiculous, because of course she would see him with other women. Unless she steered clear of every glossy magazine and skipped over the social pages of the New York papers for the rest of her life.

She picked up her pace. Did these corridors go on forever? There must be miles of them inside this palace.

Sebastian hovered so close behind her she could almost feel his body heat in the still air.

When they reached the office, she thrust her Rolodex

at him, where it sat flipped open to Pierre de Rochefauld's office number at Château D'Arc. He whipped out his phone and she rushed off to the file room that was down some stairs on the far side of the office.

She heard Sebastian greeting someone in French as she pushed deeper into the long, tunnel-like room. Thick walls rose into an arch over her head. This room must have been some kind of storage cellar in the old days. The newest paperwork was in a long metal filing cabinet in the office itself. Down here, the older papers were kept in wooden crates stacked side by side on ancient wood shelves.

Where could the Château D'Arc stuff be? There were a few token papers in the recent files, but no sign of the audits, or any hard financial data. Maybe they got buried in with the old papers?

"Tessa." Sebastian appeared in the arched doorway. He stepped down into the cramped space, and her body tingled with the urge to step toward him—and an equal but opposite urge to run for her life. His dark eyes shone in the dim light from a single, uncovered bulb. "You were right. He was there. Prickly guy, but he says he's coming to the meeting."

"Thanks for making the call." She moved her fingers through a box of files, and avoided looking at him. "I appreciate it."

He walked through the room, moved up behind her and settled his hands on her waist. He pulled her close until her backside touched the crotch of his pants. "All work and no play makes Tessa—"

"Useful." She tried to wriggle away, but his hands held her fast. "I came here to work and I'm totally embarrassed by how little I've done. I'm sure your mom isn't the only one who's noticed."

He rubbed one hand over her tummy. His broad palm heated her skin right through her smart suit. "Come on, Tessa. Let's go up on the mountain. We'll ride and then we'll…" He leaned into her and feathered a soft kiss—with warm tongue—on her neck right below her ear.

Her legs wobbled and her nipples tightened under her blouse. "I can't," she rasped. "I have to find the files." She couldn't do that again. Have the most breathtaking ride of her life, then make love to Sebastian under the sky.

Not now that she loved him. It would hurt too much. She'd start crying or begging or something.

She had no idea what she'd do. She'd never been in love before.

And already it hurt more than all the songs and poems had warned her.

"I don't want to." It was the truth.

"Why?" He stopped layering breathy kisses on her neck.

"I want to do my job for the same reasons you're going to that ceremonial dinner tonight. It's your duty, and doing it gives you a sense of satisfaction."

"Oh, Tessa." He rubbed his hands over her blouse, over her breasts and belly, then down along her thighs. "You're driving me crazy. I want you. *Now.*"

She could feel his erection hard against her backside. Feel herself growing hot and slick against him. Her face heated with the desire to kiss him. To strip his clothes off right here in the dim and dusty file room. To rub her hands over his rough thighs, and lave his hard muscle with her tongue.

Uh-oh.

This was the crazy part of her talking. The part that got her in way over her head and was now about to wrap her in a cement overcoat if she didn't save herself.

"Sebastian." She writhed against him, struggling to free herself, but only getting more aroused and dangerously unhinged in the process. Already he had her shirt untucked and his fingers roved over her bra. "Please stop."

His hand stilled. He must have noticed the pleading tone in her voice. "Last night was fun, but…not now."

"Last night was more than fun." Desire thickened his voice.

So true. Right now it was a disaster. She'd fallen in love with her boss.

For whom she was just another playful pastime.

He picked up her hair and laid it gently behind her shoulders. "I understand." He kissed her bared cheekbone. "Truly, I do. There is joy that comes with fulfilling responsibilities, and pain that comes from shirking them."

"Yes." She flipped through some files, pretending she was actually getting back to work.

He backed away. Already she felt his absence like raw skin under a freshly picked scab. "You're one in a million, Tessa."

His footsteps retreated behind her and she sank against the wooden box in front of her, heart pounding and tears rising in her throat.

One in a million, indeed. Perhaps she should feel honored to be included among the many beautiful women Sebastian had bedded.

But she didn't. She felt devastated.

Ten

Sebastian strode along the east corridor, whistling despite his uncomfortable erection. It would go away. Eventually.

Then tonight, after the Sons of the Garter dinner, he'd go to Tessa's room and they'd make love all night long.

Love. He rolled the word over his tongue, silently tasting it.

Yes. He liked it. What he felt for Tessa was totally unlike anything he'd experienced before. His heart flapped in his chest on grand eagle wings and he longed to shout his feelings from the parapets. He should laugh at himself for being so thoroughly smitten with her.

But why not? Her beauty was just the beginning. Tessa Banks was also smart, practical and determined. Energetic and enthusiastic. He loved when her green eyes sparkled with mischief. She was cheeky and fun.

An arched opening at the end of the corridor framed a

view of the harbor. He stopped and watched a fine sailboat enter through the harbor mouth.

And Tessa understood about duty.

She was the kind of woman who'd accept that she was marrying a country, as well as a man. With her by his side, he could feel himself at last transformed into a man steady and strong enough to lead his people.

And to be her husband.

"Sebastian!" A low female voice rang along the stone corridor.

Faris.

His erection withered. Sebastian managed to grunt a greeting. Her father was his dad's oldest and dearest backgammon and fishing buddy.

Shame he was also the man who'd watched Caspia Designs slide downhill over the past decade.

"Hello, my darling." Faris gathered his face in her horrible soft hands and pressed her rubbery lips to his cheek.

"What are you doing here?"

"Daddy's playing boules with your father. I came along to keep him company. I'm so glad I ran into you as I'm gasping for some sea air. You can take me out on the *Mirabella*."

"Plenty of sea air here on the balcony." He gestured to the view of the harbor.

"Oh, don't be a big grouch. Though I don't blame you for being a bit on edge after the way your secretary behaved last night."

"What are you talking about?" he growled.

"Pawing you like a rock groupie in front of everyone. So vulgar and embarrassing. But what can you expect? American girls aren't raised with any sense of propriety."

Sebastian's blood pumped with force. If Faris Maridis were a man, she'd be out cold on the hard stone by now.

"Don't you ever..." His voice was so low he could hardly hear it. "*Ever*...speak of Tessa Banks that way again." He stared right into Faris's soulless, kohl-lined eyes. "I am delighted to be the happy recipient of her affections. You are the one with no sense of propriety, insulting my guest in my own home."

Faris's long neck stiffened. "So that's how it is. Well, I'm sure you'll come to your senses sooner or later."

Sebastian battled the urge to hurl some choice insults after her, or order her off the property. But he was too well schooled in the art of diplomacy. Their families had been close allies and friends for hundreds of years and this insult was a tiny mosquito sting in the grand scheme of things.

He turned back to enjoy the view of the harbor as Faris's heels rang a brisk retreat down the corridor. His muscles stung with the urge to move, to run or fight...or make love. But he'd prove to Tessa that he could respect her wishes and keep his hands off her.

He struck out for the stables. Maybe a ride in the mountains would cool his blood.

But it didn't. Sebastian and a lathered Alto spun in agitated circles on the mountaintop, neither able to settle enough to enjoy the view. Even the ocean below seemed to heave with discontent, the sun glittering off restless peaks outside the harbor.

That night his frustration increased when the rounds of formal speeches by the Sons of the Garter continued until 2:00 a.m. Too late to disturb his lovely Tessa.

He spent an uncomfortable night aching for the soft embrace of her affectionate arms. And dreaming of the morning sunlight in her bright eyes.

"Tessa!" Sebastian's voice ricocheted off the stone columns and floors and bounced along the grand corridor.

Tessa's heart surged. But she clung tighter to the sheaf of meeting agendas in her arms. She refused to let her excitement show on her face. "Good morning, Sebastian."

He strode toward her, grabbed her and kissed her on the cheek. His lips stirred a flush of heat that spread across her face.

How could he kiss her here in front of everyone? Three of the distinguished meeting attendees stood within ten feet of her. Did he want the world to know he'd slept with his own assistant?

Maybe he didn't care. Perhaps his reputation as a playboy was a badge of pride.

"How was the Sons of the Garter dinner?" She tried to sound brisk and cheerful.

"Long." Mischief shone in his dark eyes. "Especially when there was somewhere else I'd much rather be." His steady gaze goaded the heat to her chest.

To her poor, beleaguered heart.

She sucked in a deep breath and tried to shove away the emotions barreling through her.

She'd waited for him, fear alternating with hope. *One more night, just to remember.*

Then hope turned back to fear as the hours stretched on and he still didn't come.

Maybe he's hooked up with Faris. Yes, she'd had that thought. And why not? Sebastian was anything but a faithful, one-woman man. She'd be a fool to imagine he was pining for her, too.

What did it matter why he didn't come? If he was too busy. He wasn't hers to pine for.

A gray-haired man in an expensive tweed jacket approached Tessa and she handed him an agenda with a wide smile. She wondered which of the Caspia Designs bigwigs he was.

Sebastian greeted him warmly and they spoke in French.

She didn't understand a word. And why would she? This wasn't her world. Yes, she'd been to the right school, but she'd never moved in these circles where everyone spoke five languages and was old and dear friends with everyone else.

When she realized Sebastian was introducing her, she made an effort to nod and smile. All the while wishing she could run away to hide and lick the wounds that were already so deep they'd take years to stop bleeding.

How could I have been stupid enough to let myself fall in love with him?

Tessa seemed preoccupied and Sebastian couldn't blame her. His own adrenaline ran high as he entered the meeting, flanked by the president of Carriage Leathers and the CEO of Bugaretti Fine Jewelry. The opportunity to turn these fine old companies around and increase their profitability was invigorating.

He began the meeting by inviting the business owners and executives to think outside their well-polished boxes of tradition and habit. When would Tessa make an entrance? Sergei, his father's secretary, was taking the minutes, presumably because some of the principals would be speaking in languages Tessa didn't know.

Still, he expected her to sit in. The inner workings of Caspia Designs were her business, too. Especially now that he was sketching plans to invite her into partnership of a far more permanent kind.

Lunch took place right there in the conference room—colloquially known as the War Room for its role in shaping Caspian history. Still no sign of Tessa.

While the participants drank coffee, Sebastian asked Sergei where she was. The older man glanced about the room, as if Tessa might pop out from behind a gilded column, then shrugged. Strangely anxious, Sebastian slipped out of the room and down the hall to the offices.

His spirits lifted when he saw her packing papers into the cardboard crates used to transport them to New York.

"Tessa." He said her name with a satisfied smile.

But when she looked up, her face was white, her cheeks hollow. Her magical green eyes glazed with unshed tears.

He rushed forward and took her in his arms. "What's the matter?"

"Nothing." She bit her quivering lip.

"Nonsense. Tell me." Urgency made his tone curt. "Please."

"I'm leaving as soon as the meeting is over."

Sebastian waved his hand dismissively. "Don't be ridiculous."

Her big, glittering eyes fixed on his. "I'm not."

"Tessa." He spoke her name like a chant that soothed him. He rubbed his thumb over her chin. Her lip no longer quivered and he wanted to kiss her soft mouth. "After what we've shared, I know you're not still thinking about running off to California with Paul or Peter or whatever his name is."

She trembled in his arms. "I have to go. I'm sorry I can't

fulfill my two weeks' notice but I'm sure you understand why it would not be appropriate for me to work for you any longer…under the circumstances."

The last three words were spoken in a hushed whisper.

"Sebastian! Where are you?" A masculine shout made him jerk his head around. His dad.

"I'm in the file room." He didn't release Tessa from his arms.

His dad called from the doorway. "Sergei's been looking for you. We're all ready to resume the meeting."

"I'll be right there."

Tessa's long golden lashes hid her eyes. "You must go."

"We'll talk after the meeting." He squeezed her arms. He wanted to fold her in his embrace and hold her tight.

"I won't be here." Resolve shimmered in her soft voice. Panic seized his heart. "You can't leave."

"I must go." He could see her hands were shaking.

"That's impossible." Surely he could prevent this. His ancestors would simply have forbidden her to leave.

But those days were over. Tessa was an independent-minded American—one of the many things he loved about her.

"Sebastian!" The king's voice reverberated off the stone walls. "We're all waiting."

Tessa's fingers pushed against his chest. "Sebastian, *please* go back to the meeting."

He looked deeply into her eyes. She understood about duty. She wouldn't really leave.

He'd asked her to stay and he could always count on Tessa.

He kissed her cool cheek, and released her from his arms. Then he walked away, with unease crawling over his skin.

Back in the meeting, he couldn't settle. The din of the room hurt his ears. Raised voices bounced off the marble columns and the mosaic floors. How could Tessa even think of leaving? Couldn't she see that he needed her?

He dragged his focus back to the agenda, typed by Tessa's elegant fingers. He had a meeting to lead and a company to save, and he was brought up to accept that his duty to his country must come before all other concerns.

At the end of the meeting, Sebastian rose and pushed past the meeting attendees heading for the doorway. He rushed to the office, his heart in his mouth.

But it was empty, except for the neatly stacked crates in the center of the room.

In the hallway he collared Paulo, the footman. "Where's Tessa?"

"I do not know."

"Find her!"

An ugly sensation gripped his gut. Where could she be? He marched along the hallways to her bedroom. He flung open the door, to find Anis changing the bedsheets. "Where's Tessa?"

"I think she left for the airport." The shy maid looked apologetic.

Paulo rushed into the room. "She left for the airport in a car forty minutes ago."

"Dammit!" Sebastian's shout ricocheted off the frescoed ceiling. How could she do this to him? "Get the rear gates open. Now!"

Already he raced along the passages to the garage. He could take his Land Rover through the orchards behind the palace and cut across the fields to the airport.

His father held out his arms for him as he pelted down

the main hallway. "Sebastian, where are you running to? The guests await you at the reception."

"Tessa's gone." He didn't even try to hide the panic in his voice.

"I know, son." His father grasped his arms. "Your mother arranged a private plane for her. It left five minutes ago."

"But why?"

"One cannot always understand the ways of women, my son."

"I must go after her."

"In a plane, to catch her in the skies? It's not possible."

"But I…" He didn't know what to do. This was the first time in his life that a woman had outright rejected him.

Pain seared his heart.

I love her.

He didn't say it though. Even in his distressed state he wasn't ready to confess to loving a woman who didn't love him back. He didn't wish to bring shame on the crown of Caspia.

"Duty comes first, son."

"I know, Papa, but…" Words failed him.

His father patted his cheek. "Come, eat and drink. Some things are meant to be, and some are not. Everything will look brighter in the morning."

Sebastian stumbled after him, his heart hollow with disbelief. His arms ached with the longing to hug her.

Would he never hold Tessa again?

"Sebastian, darling!" He stiffened as Faris's silvery tones rang out behind him. "Wait, sweetheart, my dress is so tight I can't walk fast. And Daddy has a walking stick, remember?"

Sebastian heard the tap of wood on stone and turned around. He didn't want to insult Faris's father. Deon Maridis had been in the meeting, and gracefully endured a harsh critique of his methods of management. Sebastian thanked the older man for his participation and help, and managed a civil greeting to Faris.

A fever of longing and despair racked his body. It was hard to talk, to be polite, when all he wanted to do was follow Tessa.

To the ends of the earth if necessary.

Faris held her father's arm tightly. She knew her family's close relationship with Sebastian's was her trump card where her prince was concerned. Sooner or later he'd see sense and realize he had to marry her.

She intended to make it sooner.

The brief conversation with her father had given her some excellent ideas.

"Sebastian, you seem awfully distracted."

"Long meeting," he grumbled.

"I think you need an evening of delicious relaxation. Perhaps a soak in the warm waters off your private dock, by candlelight? A massage with scented oils?" She waved her fingers in the air, to suggest the delicate motions she'd make on his skin.

Sebastian glanced at her hands and gave her a look of dismay.

Faris faltered. Perhaps her nails were a bit long for massage. Though honestly, she wouldn't mind shredding his flesh to ribbons the way he'd humiliated her the other night at the ball.

But at least one tiresome problem was out of the way.

She'd passed "it" in her car on the way here, and one of the palace servants had confirmed her suspicions. "I hear your assistant went back to New York in a hurry. Did she get tired of Caspia?"

"No," growled Sebastian. He looked away, tension tightening his features.

"Perhaps Caspia grew tired of her?" she purred. Quite likely Sebastian had already tired of boinking his secretary.

Sebastian's eyes flashed. "Why don't you mind your own business?"

They both glanced at her father. Mercifully he was rather deaf, but even he looked up. Sebastian nodded to him, then strode off so fast Faris didn't have a prayer of trying to catch him in her fitted dress.

What had gotten into him?

She knew exactly what had gotten into him.

She frowned, then wiped the unflattering expression away. No sense getting wrinkles over some trampy American chit.

Somehow, Tessa Banks had managed to worm her way into Sebastian's affections. And she, Faris Maridis, future Queen of Caspia, was going to flush her out.

With extreme prejudice.

Eleven

Sebastian woke up and again the hollow sense of loss hit him.

Repeated phone calls to the New York office had gone unanswered. Her cell phone was turned off.

Tessa was AWOL.

Not that he had the power to give her leave to go anywhere, now that she'd quit. He'd instructed that her last paycheck include a substantial bonus. He wanted to prove to her he didn't hold a personal grudge.

And he wanted her back.

His cell rang on the dressing table. He rubbed his face and rolled out of bed, then wearily picked it up.

"Sebastian." His father's voice made him sit up. "There's an article in the papers. Come to the dining room immediately."

Adrenaline snaked through his gut. "What's it about?"

"Just come. Now."

Sebastian pulled on pants and a shirt and slipped his feet into shoes. Could it be about Tessa?

Bad news?

He strode along the empty hallways to the dining room.

Could she be hurt? In trouble? Caught up in something she was afraid to tell him about? That would explain her strange behavior.

If that sleazy lawyer Patrick Ramsay were involved, he'd tear him limb from—

"Mama, Papa, what's the matter?" Their stricken faces stopped him dead in the doorway.

His father tapped the paper in front of him. "The participants of the meeting were sworn to secrecy, were they not?"

Sebastian strode into the room. "Yes. They all signed a confidentiality agreement."

"Then how do you explain *this*?" He pointed to an article near the bottom of the page.

Sebastian grabbed the paper and scanned it.

Caspia Designs Mired in Debt and Mismanagement.

He sucked in a breath as he read. The article was brief. A single column, laying bare the company's recent stagnation and the sliding profits of its component parts. It mentioned large debts recently incurred by Château D'Arc wineries. And the final paragraph outlined a problem that Sebastian had never mentioned outside the meeting—not even to Reed—that the company was plagued by decades of uncollectible accounts, amounting to a potential write-off of more than three million dollars.

He could barely focus on the tiny words.

"Tessa Banks uncovered all those debts, didn't she?" Sebastian's mother took a sip of her coffee.

"There wasn't much to uncover. They were sitting right there in the books. Deon Maridis had been letting accounts receivable slide for years."

His father leaned forward. "Deon saw them as debts from personal friends. Good people who'd pay eventually."

"But they won't, will they?" asked his mom.

"Some of our oldest customers aren't as rich as they used to be." The king sighed and leaned back in his chair. "They rested on their laurels too long just like Caspia Designs. That didn't stop them buying jewels and champagne they couldn't afford, though."

"What would happen if you tried to collect through professionals?" His mom lifted her coffee cup.

Sebastian and his dad stared at her in horror. The king almost rose from his chair. "Shame our friends with lawsuits and public humiliation? Never. I'd pay their debts myself first."

The queen's eyebrows rose. "I hope that won't be necessary."

Sebastian put the paper on the table. "These debts won't matter in the long run. We'll write them off and get the businesses humming the way they should be. Profits will be back up within the year."

His dad clapped his hands together. "Thank heaven we've got Sebastian in on the game to shake things up."

"This article will cause the stock to move, though." Sebastian glanced back at the paper. "And it won't be going up." He whipped his PDA out of his pocket and pulled up his ticker symbols.

An ancient tribal curse fell from his lips.

His father tapped the paper. "Who could have let this leak out? I'd stake my life on the good faith of our principals."

"Pierre de Rochefauld was rather evasive." Sebastian remembered the dismal accounting ledgers Tessa had unearthed on the ancient and unprofitable Château D'Arc wineries. "And he wasn't happy when I read him the riot act for getting his winery into debt this year to pay for repairs to his château."

"But would he want his own debts publicized in an international paper?" His father shook his head. "I think not."

His mother waved her hand dismissively. "I agree with your father. They were all such charming gentlemen. Even the girl from Carriage Leathers was delightful."

"She's not a girl, Mama. She's at least your age."

His mother narrowed her eyes. "What are you implying, Sebastian?"

Sebastian rubbed his temples.

"I know you're fond of Tessa Banks…" His father's soft tone made him look up. "But what do we really know about her?"

Tessa pulled another long strip of packing tape and ripped it off with a loud rasp. She'd well and truly mucked up her life. Now she had to move on whether she wanted to or not.

She'd given notice on her apartment before she left for Caspia and it was already rented for the following month. She had to be out by the end of the day or lose her deposit.

She smoothed the tape over the flaps holding a box shut. Lucky thing she had so little stuff. She could stow it in her parents' basement until she figured out a game plan.

Which was a challenge, since the first thing she'd done when she got back was tell Patrick she wasn't moving to California with him.

Heat crept up her neck in shame at how she'd betrayed him. Cheated on him after only a couple of days in Sebastian's company. She deserved everything that fell on her now.

She hadn't told Patrick what really happened. Just that she'd had a "change of heart." She hadn't even had the guts to tell him face-to-face.

Oddly he'd sounded almost relieved. Maybe he somehow knew she was an unreliable and untrustworthy partner.

And her job at Caspia Designs was history. Even if Sebastian did want to keep her on—she was an efficient and experienced worker, after all—she'd rather be honorably dead than sit there typing his memos while fielding phone calls from his newest girl-of-the-week.

She slumped for a moment and rested her forehead on the cool cardboard of the packing carton. She cut herself some slack by acknowledging she'd had no chance. He was Sebastian. She was doomed the moment he decided to flirt with her.

Her heart still squeezed when she remembered the warmth and passion she'd seen in his dark eyes. Of course it had just been lust, but…

"Oh, dammit all to hell!" She pounded her fist on the box. It would have been so much easier to get on with the rest of her life if she hadn't royally screwed up this part.

No pun intended.

He hadn't called. What had she expected? Besides, she'd mailed her cell phone back to the office. She didn't want him thinking she'd try to sneak any "free perks" on account of their intimacy.

Her door was ajar in a vain attempt to create a cross breeze in her top-floor apartment, and she heard footsteps on the stairs. Tessa frowned. The Man-With-Van wasn't due for another hour. Besides, she hadn't buzzed anyone up, and her neighbors were all at work. "Who's there?"

She sprang to her feet as the door swung open.

"What's the matter?" Sebastian materialized in the doorway.

Her mouth fell open.

"I heard you cry out. Are you okay?" He looked around, taking in all the boxes. The ugly mess that was her upended life.

"Um, sure. I'm fine." She cringed that he'd heard her curse.

Her heart pounded. He'd come after her. Did this mean...?

Hope faded as she looked at him. Tension tightened his hard features and knotted the muscles under his dark gray T-shirt.

An awkward silence thickened the air.

"Are you responsible for the leak to the *Wall Street Journal?*" His black gaze bore into her.

Tessa shrank back. "What? I don't know what you're talking about."

Sebastian's eyes narrowed. "Apart from the principals at the meeting, who all signed a confidentiality agreement, you are the only person who was privy to the most recent financial details. Even the auditors haven't seen them yet."

"And you think I leaked them to the press? I would never do that." Horror soaked through her. He thought she was capable of that kind of betrayal?

She swallowed hard and forced back sharp tears.

Obviously their kisses, their caresses had meant less than nothing to him.

And they'd meant *so much* to her.

He glanced around her apartment. "Moving, I see."

"Yes." She could barely get the word out. She needed him out of here *now*, before she started bawling. "I didn't leak the information and I have packing to do. Could you please leave?"

Her voice quavered on the last word, dangerously close to a sob. Sebastian's expression softened for a moment, then closed over again. Hard and rigid.

He backed toward the door, perhaps unwilling to take his eyes off her because he didn't know what she'd try next.

She held herself steady, lifted her chin. Dared him to believe what he wanted about her.

His unrelenting gaze made her knees tremble, as it always had. But this time a claw of sadness gripped her heart.

He turned and left the room.

Tessa sagged, barely able to stay on her feet as she watched him head for the stairs.

She knew it was just a fling. A stupid fling. A mistake.

Her carefully planned future with Patrick might not have been filled with sweaty nights of passion, but it could have brought the joys of children and family life. That was a dream that might have actually come true.

But now? She'd chucked it all away to fall madly in love with a man who thought so little of her that he believed she'd betray him and his company.

A loud, ugly sob flew from her mouth.

Did he think she was out for revenge?

Perhaps she should want revenge for how he'd seduced her. She felt so broken now. Something had been taken from her, something she never knew she had until Sebastian found it deep in her.

The capacity for sheer joy.

Now that she'd lain in Sebastian's arms, her body intertwined with his hard muscle, her mind and soul aloft with bliss, she'd never be happy with an ordinary "relationship" again.

Sebastian crashed down the stairs, his heart racing.

He had a hard time thinking straight after he saw those boxes. Tessa was packing to move to California, exactly as she'd planned.

He'd planned to greet her warmly, win her back. Until he saw that she'd already moved on. Left him behind, part of her old life.

He hadn't meant to rudely accuse her, but the pain of seeing her preparing for her new life without him had cut him to the quick and made fresh, poisonous doubts spring into his mind.

She'd denied leaking the information, but she'd seemed tense, strung out...*afraid.*

Like someone who'd done something they shouldn't have.

He thumped his hand on the metal railing and cursed the hot wave of desire that had crashed through him at the sight of her face. Of her long, lean body encased in faded jeans and a skimpy white tank top.

His chest ached, too. He'd climbed the stairs on a crest of anticipation and adrenaline, footsteps springing with hope and excitement at the prospect of seeing Tessa again.

But those emerald eyes had greeted him with suspicion. With hostility.

An ugly curse flew from his lips as he bolted out into the hot, late-September-afternoon sun of the Brooklyn street. His limo was parked up the block and he stalked over to it in the foulest mood of his life.

How could he have been so wrong about her? He'd dreamed of making her his future queen. Of sharing his life with her.

Was she angry he'd forced her to stay when she wanted to go to California? Was she upset that he'd seduced her?

He slammed the limo door and fell against the seat. "Back to Park Avenue." His driver had the tact not to turn around or inquire after his activities.

Sebastian clenched his fists as regret soaked through him. He'd coaxed Tessa into bed while she was an employee and he had authority over her. And when he knew that she was involved with another man.

Maybe she had good reason to be angry.

He could have handled things differently.

No, he couldn't. He'd been completely besotted by her. Common sense didn't stand a chance when he saw the Caspian sun dance in her golden hair and heard her laughter mingle with birdsong high on the mountaintop.

He held his head in his hands.

Tessa was still leaving for California with another man.

Sebastian's first experience with total rejection hurt like a crushing blow to his chest. His natural instinct was to fight back, to slay his opponent and emerge victorious in the tradition of his ancestors.

But he was wise enough to know that no true victory came from sheer force.

The phone was ringing as he shoved open the door to his apartment at 721 Park Avenue. He walked right past the phone on the foyer table, slammed into the kitchen and poured himself a glass of water, waiting for the machine to pick up.

Incessantly it rang, pounding his aching brain. The machine must be full. That happened sometimes when there was no one around to check it. Now he needed a new house sitter *and* a new assistant. Was there no one he could depend on?

He marched back into the foyer, picked up the receiver and barked, "What?"

"Sebastian, darling."

Faris. He narrowly resisted the urge to slam the phone down. It was probably she who had filled the machine, though, so he might as well find out what she wanted and get her out of his hair.

"I heard how your former assistant leaked proprietary information to the *Wall Street Journal.* I'm just sick about it! You think you know people, but you can't trust anyone these days. It's so hard to find good staff."

Sebastian's tongue twitched with words that might have flown off it if he weren't so used to representing his nation in everything he said and did.

"We don't know who leaked the information." He hated Faris gloating over Tessa's betrayal. It fomented something ugly and painful in his gut.

"Oh, come on, darling! I know you had a bit of a soft spot for her, but really. They probably threw some money at her and she blabbed it all."

"I hardly think the *Wall Street Journal* is offering cash for tip-offs."

"All those proprietary details. Shocking! I do hope she doesn't spill any other more *personal* information to the press." Her smarmy tone made his back stiffen.

"Tessa would never do that." His voice rumbled with conviction that he truly felt.

"Still defending her? Oh, sweetheart, I'd better fly out there and kiss you all better."

"Please don't." He ended the call, his flesh crawling at the prospect of Faris's lip-gloss-drenched kisses.

Something still gnawed at him.

And it wasn't anything as transient as lust.

It was doubt.

Could Tessa really have leaked company information? He couldn't truly accept the idea. Defending her came as naturally as breathing.

Probably because he was such a sucker for her.

He slammed the phone into its cradle on the hall table, which caused a cascade amongst the mail piled there. Envelopes, cards and junk mail slid down onto the parquet floor.

He bent to grab a handful of it, and something caught his eye.

An envelope. A slim beige rectangle. Nothing strange about it, except that it looked eerily familiar.

He slit it open with his thumb.

Black ink crawled over the pages like a drunken spider. "Sebastian darling, I…" He crumpled it and was about to throw it on the floor when that gnawing sensation in his gut turned into sharp claws.

He unfolded the paper with the same revulsion he'd felt at the dining table in Caspia when he opened an identical envelope with an identical piece of paper inside it.

Different writing. Same person.

He let the paper and his hand fall to the table and he leaned on it for a moment. Faris had written him that sleazy, threatening note telling him not to marry a foreign bride and insulting Tessa by name.

That truly surprised him. He wouldn't have thought even Faris capable of something quite so vulgar.

What else might she try?

The spore of suspicion mushroomed in his brain. Her father was in the meeting about Caspia Designs. Faris could easily have teased some details about the company out of him.

Another thought soaked into his cortex. The article had very specific information about Château D'Arc and its disastrous recent debts. No doubt the reason Pierre de Rochefauld had been so reluctant to show his face at the meeting.

But Tessa didn't know about the new debts. They didn't come up until late in the afternoon.

After she'd already left.

A fierce surge of adrenaline stung Sebastian's muscles. He was going to the offices of the *Wall Street Journal* right now to find out the source of this information.

As he strode through the lobby of his building, mind racing, he almost knocked right into his neighbor Amanda Crawford. The lively event planner was tall, blond and beautiful.

But she wasn't Tessa.

He managed a friendly greeting and a kiss on the cheek.

She gave him a faux-stern look. "I don't think I ever got your RSVP for our party celebrating the landmark status of this old heap." She gestured around the glittering marbled space of the lobby.

"Oh, yeah." He grimaced. "Sorry, my mail is a disaster as I haven't been here much. Carrie quit and I don't have a new house sitter yet. I saw the invite in the mess, though. I'll be sure to come if I'm in the country."

Amanda leaned into him, her gray eyes twinkling with mischief. "Lucky thing you're so lovable, Sebastian. You already missed the party. But never mind about that, you've also missed the juiciest gossip of the decade while you were away. The police seem to think that Marie Endicott's death was a homicide."

Sebastian froze. "You're kidding." Marie was the younger sister of his friend Drew from boarding school. He'd known her as a cute, curly-haired pest, then later as a successful woman with her own real-estate firm. She'd lived in the building for a while, until one day she jumped off the roof. An apparent suicide.

Amanda grabbed his arm. "Not kidding. Apparently there are tapes of the incident. From security cameras on the roof. I guess they prevent burglars sneaking in from adjoining buildings or something. But the tapes have gone missing."

Sebastian's chest tightened. "That's terrible. Who would kill Marie?"

"That's what everyone wants to know. Bizarre, isn't it?" Her conspiratorial whisper chilled his blood.

How did such terrible things happen? His heart went out to her brother and parents. "I hope they catch whoever did it. Let me know if there's anything I can do to help."

"It's shocking how many crimes go unsolved in this city." Amanda shook her head.

He bid her goodbye, cursing the harm cruel people inflict on others.

I know one crime that won't go unsolved.

Sebastian wasn't leaving the newspaper offices until he uncovered the source of the leak.

Twelve

Sebastian flew out of the *Wall Street Journal* offices on a wave of excitement.

A staffer told him the story was put together at the European office in Brussels, where one of Sebastian's oldest friends worked as an editor. Sebastian got his friend on the phone, he'd talked to the reporter, and within minutes he had all the information he needed. He didn't even have to ask them to reveal their source.

Faris had leaked the information.

Keeping calm, Sebastian offered a story on how he intended to turn the companies around within the year. He talked to a New York reporter for more than an hour about Caspia Designs and its challenges and prospects for the future, until Sebastian excused himself on the pretext of urgent business.

Very urgent business.

He jumped into his waiting limo and slammed the door. "Tessa's apartment in Brooklyn, and hurry!"

Tessa had nothing to do with the story. The reporter confirmed that he had never heard of her.

Sebastian's heart threatened to beat right out of his chest as he thought of the way he'd cruelly accused her and refused to take her word for her innocence. He wouldn't be able to eat or sleep until he'd offered her his most profound apologies.

But she wasn't there.

Repeated ringing on the doorbell followed by calling up to the open windows brought one of her neighbors to the door. The bearded young man explained that she'd moved out, with all her belongings, about two hours earlier.

She'd left no forwarding address.

Cursing, Sebastian figured he'd earned the humiliation of tracking her down at Patrick Ramsay's. It didn't take long to find out where the divorce-lawyer-to-the-stars kept his private office, and Sebastian pulled up in front of the midtown brownstone intent on a dignified and gentlemanly exchange.

As he climbed out of the car, the man in question appeared at the top of the wide stairs, wearing a gray pinstriped suit and carrying a furled umbrella.

Sebastian squared his shoulders. "I'd like to see Tessa."

Pale eyes squinted at him. "Who are you?"

"Sebastian Stone. I'm her…" His heart yearned to say "I'm her lover" but he held himself in check. "I'm her former employer."

"Oh, right. The *prince*." His tone of derision caused Sebastian's hackles to rise.

Still, this was the man Tessa had chosen. He held himself steady. "May I speak with her, please?"

"You may speak with whomever you like. You won't find her here, though."

"Where is she?"

"Hell if I know. I got a Dear John phone call a few days ago. Just as well, as I've been offered a big new case here in New York and won't be able to make the move we'd discussed. I assume she told you that we were—"

"Yes." Sebastian cut him off before he could use any unpleasant descriptive phrases. A ray of hope flashed through him as the lawyer's words sank into his brain. "She broke off with you?"

"Yes. Ironic, really, since a week ago she was hinting about marriage and all that jazz. Hardly my cup of tea when I spend all day rending asunder what the good Lord has joined together." He laughed.

Sebastian clenched his fists. "Where do you think she went?"

"No idea. For all I know, she went to California without me."

Panic flashed through Sebastian.

"I doubt it, though," Patrick continued. "She didn't know anyone there and she's not the type to jump off a precipice." He leaned toward Sebastian. "She's a sweet girl. You will give her job back if she asks, won't you?"

"Yes," Sebastian rasped, slightly revising his opinion of Ramsay.

But I hope to give her so much more.

He headed to where his limo idled in an illegal parking space. As they drove back to Park Avenue, he tried to rack his mind for someone who might know where Tessa would be. Maybe if he combed through the Rolodex she'd recently reorganized for him, he'd come up with something.

He'd left her on the brink of tears, devastated that he thought her a traitor to the company.

He'd assumed her behavior sprang from guilt. Now he was sure—so sure—that it came from the pain of seeing his lack of faith in her.

He crashed through the doors of 721 Park Avenue with such force that the women waiting for the elevator swung around to see what all the commotion was. Carrie and Julia.

Carrie waved. "Hi, Sebastian." His former house sitter looked radiant with happiness. She still lived in the building with her husband, Trent Tanford. Sebastian held Trent personally responsible for his own overloaded answering machine and teetering stacks of mail.

Still, he didn't begrudge Carrie her happiness. He kissed her on both cheeks. "Marriage appears to be treating you well."

"It is. And we're getting married again." She blushed.

"Already? To whom?" He raised an eyebrow and tried not to grin.

"Each other, of course. But our last wedding was kind of…rushed. This time we're going to make it perfect." Her eyes sparkled. "You will come, won't you?"

"I can never resist a wedding." Sebastian did enjoy weddings, with their promise of a bright future and children and the continuation of life's cycle. All Caspians loved weddings.

His heart squeezed.

If he could just find Tessa and convince her to marry him.

"Do you notice something different about Julia?"

"What?" Carrie's words tugged him back to the present. He scanned Julia. He'd heard that the former resident of his building had married Wall Street whiz Max Rolland a couple of months ago. She'd moved into his place just a block or so away. Julia looked lovely as always, her blue eyes shining and her skin glowing with good health. Perhaps a little plumper than usual, but he wasn't idiotic enough to say that.

Julia laughed. "I'm pregnant, Sebastian. Five months, in fact, so don't worry about noticing my expanded girth."

"Congratulations." He kissed her on both cheeks, and again for luck. His heart tugged again. "Your baby will bring you and Max so much joy."

Joy he wanted to share with Tessa.

Pain sent a surge of adrenaline spearing through him. He grabbed Carrie's arm. "Carrie, you and Tessa were friends, weren't you?"

"Sure. What's up?"

"I must find her. She quit her job and now she's moved out of her apartment. She left no forwarding address and I…" Words failed him as he scanned her face, hoping she could help.

Understanding dawned in Carrie's sharp and compassionate eyes. "I think she said something about going to her parents' house in Connecticut until she finds a new place. They live in Stamford. I have the address upstairs. Come on up and I'll give it to you."

Sebastian drove his own car to Stamford. He didn't want a driver idling nearby, glancing at his watch. Even his Alfa Romeo seemed wound-up and jumpy, and the traffic on I-95 ratcheted his blood pressure higher as the day stretched into late afternoon.

What if she wasn't there? He'd thought about calling but decided not to. If he were Tessa, he'd slam the phone down on himself.

What he had to say could only be said face-to-face.

He hated GPS, but as he drove into the labyrinth of the old coastal city he turned it on and punched in her address. Neat brick pseudo mansions lined clean, quiet streets. Already he found himself scanning the sidewalks for signs of Tessa.

He turned again, onto a sloping street of older wooden houses, and again into a street of modest homes facing a weedy basketball court.

Sebastian snapped to attention. Basketball. Could this be her old neighborhood? There were people on the streets and he was tempted to stop and ask about Tessa, but the GPS told him to keep driving, so he pushed onward.

It finally brought him to a stop in front of a tiny, mint-green cottage, surrounded by a chain-link fence. A huge oak tree towered over the tiny structure, shading out all possibility of grass in the postage-stamp-sized lot.

Tessa grew up here? When she'd said she came from a modest background, he'd imagined an ordinary suburban home with a grassy yard and a large dog. And a garden shed the size of this house.

But as he stepped out of the car and rounded the oak tree he saw a familiar slender form, bent at the waist, her tempting backside jutting toward him.

Joy surged through him. "Tessa."

She glanced up, startled. She held a paintbrush between her teeth, and quickly removed it as she registered his presence. A can of red paint sat on the sidewalk. She unbent herself to reveal a half-painted metal mailbox.

Then she went back to painting it.

She didn't say anything at all.

Sebastian approached her, his heart so full it could burst. "Tessa, I'm here to offer my most humble apologies. I know you didn't leak the story and I should never have accused you. I'm sorry from the bottom of my heart."

She didn't look up. He thought for a second that her hand trembled, but it kept moving, making strokes of red paint over the battered metal of the mailbox.

An emotional outpouring of Caspian words flooded his brain, but he forced himself to slow down and think in English.

"Faris leaked the story. I suspect she did it to come between you and me."

Her hand paused in its brushing motion, muscles tight. "It really doesn't matter who leaked the story." She stared at the mailbox. "I don't even care if you believe it was me. It won't make any difference in the long run. You'll turn the company around and everything will be fine."

Her voice was flat. Lifeless. Her hair was pulled back in a ponytail and loose strands fell to cover her face, hiding her from him. The air had cooled and she wore a gray sweatshirt, but he could still see the tension in her neck and shoulders.

Was she afraid to turn and look at him?

Pain jerked through him and he stepped forward and grabbed her arm holding the brush.

She felt warm and alive, and already sweet relief cascaded through him. *He'd found her.*

When she glanced up, her wide green eyes brimmed

with tears. Distress shadowed her lovely features and her usual glow had dimmed almost out of existence.

His chest constricted. "I'm so, so sorry." The words fell from his lips. Almost meaningless. They weren't the words he wanted to say. That he needed to say.

"You're on my mind day and night. My flesh aches for you and my heart craves you close." His voice trembled as hope and longing overflowed.

She blinked, startled. Two fat sparkling tears rolled from her beautiful eyes.

He reached up and brushed one away with his thumb. He inhaled deeply.

This was no time for caution or royal dignity.

"I love you, Tessa, and I can't live without you."

Tessa blinked rapidly, trying to clear her eyes. She couldn't see through the mist of tears and she wanted to make sure she was really awake and right here on the planet earth. She barely believed this scene could exist outside of her imagination.

Sebastian's face hovered inches in front of hers, his forehead creased with concern and his dark, expressive eyes fixed on hers.

I love you.

Surely she hadn't heard those words. But they echoed in her ears, off the great oak tree, off the faded aluminum siding of the house behind her.

Her stunned silence seemed to encourage him. He took her hand in his. The warmth of his touch was like a shot of adrenaline to her heart, which kicked inside her chest.

Painful.

He raised her hands and kissed her knuckles. Which,

she noticed with embarrassment, were smeared with red paint.

"Each day without you has shown me how much I want you in my life. How much I need you." His intense, dark gaze stole her breath. "I know you ended your relationship with Patrick and I…I beg you to come home with me. I want you by my side, every day, for the rest of my life."

Tessa's mind swam as shivers of amazement skittered over her flesh. *Could he really mean it?*

The sound of a car horn a block away yanked her back to the present. To the tiny front yard with its chipped mailbox. The ordinary street with its motley collection of the least-valuable real estate in Stamford.

She gestured around her. "Sebastian, this is where I come from. I'm not royal, or aristocratic, or any of the things you'd need in a…partner."

She didn't say the word *wife*. He hadn't asked her to marry him.

"Where you come from doesn't matter. I come from Caspia and I'm in love with an American woman. Nothing is more natural than two people falling in love. You and I are meant to be together. I know it in my soul."

He squeezed her hands and the truth of his words echoed in her heart.

The screech of hinges made her glance up to see her mother in the doorway of the house.

"What's going on out here, dear?" Her mom came out of the doorway and down the single step.

Tessa tugged her hands and Sebastian released them. "Um, Mom, this is Sebastian Stone. He's my…boss." Her face heated. "My former boss."

Sebastian strode forward, past the paint can and up the

cracked front walk. He looked huge in the minuscule front yard. He also towered over her tiny, gray-haired mom, who pulled her sweater about her to ward off a sudden September chill.

He held out his hand. "Mrs. Banks, it's an honor to meet you."

"Sebastian Stone...the prince?"

He bowed slightly. "At your service, madam."

"Well." Her mom smiled, a flush lighting her smooth cheeks. "Tessa has told us a lot about you. She had a lovely time visiting your country and I told her she was silly to leave her good job."

Tessa swallowed.

"I think she was absolutely right to quit." Sebastian's voice rang out in the quiet neighborhood.

Tessa froze.

"I've been wasting her talents on filing and office duties, when she's capable of so much more."

He took her mother's hand in both of his. "Mrs. Banks, did you ever think of moving to a warmer, more cheerful climate?"

Her mom hesitated, looking confused, then turned back into the house. "Harry, come here, dear."

Tessa shoved a hand through her hair, which wasn't a good idea since it was in a ponytail and her hand had paint on it. Her heart thudded so loud she was sure they could hear it. What on earth was Sebastian doing?

Her father shuffled forward, using a walker because of his advanced osteoarthritis. He hesitated at the step, and Tessa moved to help him down, but Sebastian beat her to it, offering his strong arm for support.

Her mom patted her dad's arm. "Harry, it's Tessa's

boss. The prince." She hissed the last word as if it was some kind of hint.

"Pleased to meet you, young man."

Tessa smiled as her dad's rich, self-confident voice echoed in the air. He wasn't intimidated by anything, least of all royalty. He and Sebastian shook hands. "My daughter tells me you have a beautiful country."

"Caspia is indeed the loveliest place on earth. I think you'd like it very much if you were to visit."

"I don't doubt it. We're dreading another winter. I can feel its teeth already. We're trying to figure out how to move to Florida." Her father laughed.

"Caspia is warm and dry year-round, and we treasure people of mature years for their wisdom and experience."

Tessa's eyes widened.

"We have the highest life expectancy of any country on earth, so you can tell we take good care of our older citizens. If you were to move to Caspia for your golden years, you would find the climate salubrious and the people most friendly and welcoming."

"It does sound pleasant." Her father smiled and glanced at Tessa, obviously as perplexed as she was. "We'd better leave you two young people to your business, right, dear?" He winked at her mother.

Tessa gulped. She stayed rooted in place while her dad shuffled back inside with her mother fussing over him.

Once the door was closed, she put her hands on her hips. "What's going on?"

Sebastian marched back toward her and took her hands again. Excitement sparkled in his eyes. "If you're moving to Caspia, your parents must come, too."

"What are you talking about?"

He looked amused. "I'm proposing to you, of course."

Proposing what, exactly? Her heart beat so fast and hard she couldn't speak. Which was fine, as she had no idea what to say.

Sebastian pulled a ring off his little finger.

Tessa gulped. *Was he—?*

He eased himself down so that one knee rested on the concrete pavers of the front walk.

Blood rushed to her brain and she found herself gasping for breath.

Sebastian bent his head for a moment, then looked up at her. "Tessa, I wish to spend the rest of my life by your side. I've been waiting all my life for you. I know you're the woman who was born to be my queen one day."

Her legs grew shaky. *Queen?*

"I promise to be a caring and faithful husband and a loving father to our children."

Children? Her heart squeezed.

"I wish for you to have the happy life you were prepared to move to an unknown city for, except I wish to share it with you in Caspia."

Tears gathered in her eyes again. She couldn't help it. It was too perfect, too wonderful.

Sebastian cleared his throat. He looked into her eyes with a gaze so filled with emotion that it stole her breath. "Tessa Banks, will you be my wife?"

The words, thick with feeling, shuddered through her and shook her to her core.

But no response came to her lips.

It was too good to be true. It couldn't be real.

She shook her head, trying to scatter the thoughts that crowded her like gulls at a beach picnic.

Sebastian took her hand, and for a moment she thought he was going to force the ring onto her trembling fingers.

But he didn't. He squeezed her hand gently and rubbed her palm with his thumb. Then he stood and closed his warm, strong arms around her shaking shoulders.

"I love you, Tessa. Maybe I'm coming on too strong and trying to rush you too much. It's okay if you're not ready to agree right now. Being a queen is not something everyone aspires to."

Queen? She'd forgotten about that part. Of course she couldn't marry him. He'd come to his senses and realize what a horrible mistake he'd made soon enough.

"I can't be a queen." Her voice sounded high and thin as she admitted her failing. "I know I sound like one of your crowd because I went to St. Peter's, but deep inside I'll always be Tessa Banks, from right here."

The lowering sun threw unflattering harsh shadows over the less-than-elegant surroundings. A group of kids on their way home from school called out to them, whistling and laughing.

Sebastian resisted her attempt to pull away and tugged her closer. "I know you will always be Tessa Banks, from right here." His eyes shone. "That's one of the many things I love about you. You're down-to-earth and practical and you don't expect to have life handed to you on a silver platter. You're warm and funny and brave and beautiful, and I love you exactly as you are." He stroked her cheek, making her skin hum. "We'll share a good life together."

Oh, dear. Tears filled her eyes again. The worst part was that she believed him. She could so easily picture a full and happy life with Sebastian: nights in his embrace, days in the beautiful Caspian countryside, children running along the palace corridors, breakfast in the royal dining room...

With the king and queen.

That splash of cold reality snapped her back to her senses. "Sebastian, I'm sure you would be a fantastic husband and father, but there are a lot of people who'd be very unhappy to see us married. Your mother, for example."

Sebastian pressed his face into her neck, which sent a rush of heat flooding through her. "Don't worry about my mother. She can be silly and snobbish sometimes, but it's just the way she was brought up. She's a good person at heart. I know you won't believe me now, but I think the two of you will be close friends one day."

Tessa wanted to laugh. He spoke of the future, so certain it would happen. Her doubts were irrelevant.

How could you not love that kind of confidence?

"My father adores you." He nuzzled her gently. "He offered his full approval of any intentions I had toward you."

Tessa jerked back. "You told him you had intentions toward me?"

"No, but I guess it was written all over my face and he wanted to let me know it was okay."

"I guess that was before you all decided that I leaked the story." She narrowed her eyes.

"No, it was after." He grinned. "I guess that's when Dad knew I was really serious about you. I didn't believe the leak could be you until I came to your apartment and found you packing up—to move away with another man, I thought—and you were so nervous and evasive. I didn't know what to think, except that I was losing you."

Tessa let out something between a laugh and a sob. "I couldn't stand to be near you in case you found out how crazy I am about you. I was so humiliated by being in love with you when I thought I was just another notch on your royal bedpost."

Sebastian threw his head back and laughed. "You do love me, too! I knew it."

She cocked her head. "No one could accuse you of lacking self-assurance."

"True, true. But I must assure you that those notches on my bedpost date back to an entirely different generation. Somewhere around the late sixteenth century, we think." His eyes glittered with mischief.

"I guess that's a liability of hanging on to used furniture."

His mouth fought a smile. "Caspians are practical people. We're satisfied with the best of everything and we don't give it up easily." He pulled back a little. His dark eyes looked at her steadily. "I know you fell in love with Caspia, as well as with me."

"You make me sound so promiscuous." She tried to laugh, but his serious gaze demanded a real answer. "Yes, I did. I'd never dreamed such a magical place could exist. I confess I've missed Caspia almost as much as I've missed you."

"Your parents would be happy there."

Her chest tightened. How typical of Sebastian to make plans for everyone. "It was thoughtful of you to consider them."

"I'm Caspian. Family is the foundation of our culture." His gaze softened. "And I wish for you and I to create the next generation together."

It was lucky Sebastian held her tight, or she might have collapsed into a swoon and cracked her skull on the concrete. Too many dreams coming true all at once could be dangerous for a girl.

"Your role as queen will not always be easy, since being a monarch does come with responsibilities, but I know you're resourceful enough to handle your role with grace and ease."

She bit her lip. Put like that, as a *job,* even being queen did seem…doable. She was nothing if not a hard worker. She blew out a long, shaky breath.

"Let's try this again." Sebastian loosened his hold on her, and lifted the hand holding the ring. "Tessa Banks, will you be my wife?"

She stared at the ring, a gold hoop scrolled with vines. "Yes." She stared into his dark eyes. Passion shone there, and love, and the promise of the joy they could share. "Yes. I will."

He slid the ring onto her ring finger. Her skin tingled as the cool metal settled into place. The ring was far too big, but somehow it felt exactly right.

Sebastian gathered her in his arms and kissed her with a desperate urgency that echoed her own. Desire and hope crackled through her with electric force.

She clung to him, to his sturdy strength, as the fear and hurt and sadness that had hounded her home from Caspia wafted away on the late-afternoon breeze.

She'd hoped for a loving husband to create a family with. Little did she know she'd been working with him for nearly five years.

She knew Sebastian so well that of course she loved him. She'd dreamed of touching him, of kissing him, of being held in his arms, but she'd never dared to dream of sharing her life with him.

Her dreams and reality had crashed into each other with explosive force, lighting up a future brighter than anything she could have imagined.

Sebastian's tongue sent shivers of excitement chasing through her. Resisting the urge to writhe against him, she opened her eyes. "Hey, I have a reputation to protect in this neighborhood."

"You're not allowed to kiss your husband?"

She stared at him. "When you put it that way, I guess it's okay."

His lips settled back over hers as his powerful arms held her close. Warmth and pleasure suffused her whole body, until she floated on a cloud of joy.

She still felt like Tessa Banks, from right here.

Except that now she was the happiest woman on earth.

* * * * *

Turn the page for a sneak preview of
AFTERSHOCK, *a new anthology*
featuring New York Times *bestselling author*
Sharon Sala.

Available October 2008.

n●cturne™

Dramatic and sensual tales of paranormal romance.

Chapter 1

October
New York City

Nicole Masters was sitting cross-legged on her sofa while a cold autumn rain peppered the windows of her fourth-floor apartment. She was poking at the ice cream in her bowl and trying not to be in a mood.

Six weeks ago, a simple trip to her neighborhood pharmacy had turned into a nightmare. She'd walked into the middle of a robbery. She never even saw the man who shot her in the head and left her for dead. She'd survived, but some of her senses had not. She was dealing with short-term memory loss and a tendency to stagger. Even though she'd been told the problems were most likely temporary, she waged a daily battle with depression.

Her parents had been killed in a car wreck when she was twenty-one. And except for a few friends—and most recently her boyfriend, Dominic Tucci, who lived in the apartment right above hers, she was alone. Her doctor kept reminding her that she should be grateful to be alive, and on one level she knew he was right. But he wasn't living in her shoes.

If she'd been anywhere else but at that pharmacy when the robbery happened, she wouldn't have died twice on the way to the hospital. Instead of being grateful that she'd survived, she couldn't stop thinking of what she'd lost.

But that wasn't the end of her troubles. On top of everything else, something strange was happening inside her head. She'd begun to hear odd things: sounds, not voices—at least, she didn't think it was voices. It was more like the distant noise of rapids—a rush of wind and water inside her head that, when it came, blocked out everything around her. It didn't happen often, but when it did, it was frightening, and it was driving her crazy.

The blank moments, which is what she called them, even had a rhythm. First there came that sound, then a cold sweat, then panic with no reason. Part of her feared it was the beginning of an emotional breakdown. And part of her feared it wasn't—that it was going to turn out to be a permanent souvenir of her resurrection.

Frustrated with herself and the situation as it stood, she upped the sound on the TV remote. But instead of *Wheel of Fortune,* an announcer broke in with a special bulletin.

"This just in. Police are on the scene of a kidnapping that occurred only hours ago at The Dakota. Molly Dane, the six-year-old daughter of one of Holly-wood's blockbuster stars, Lyla Dane, was taken by force from the family apartment. At this time they have yet to receive a ransom demand. The house-keeper was seriously injured during the abduction, and is, at the present time, in surgery. Police are hoping to be able to talk to her once she regains con-sciousness. In the meantime, we are going now to a press conference with Lyla Dane."

Horrified, Nicole stilled as the cameras went live to where the actress was speaking before a bank of micro-phones. The shock and terror in Lyla Dane's voice were physically painful to watch. But even though Nicole kept upping the volume, the sound continued to fade.

Just when she was beginning to think something was wrong with her set, the broadcast suddenly switched from the Dane press conference to what appeared to be footage of the kidnapping, beginning with footage from inside the apartment.

When the front door suddenly flew back against the wall and four men rushed in, Nicole gasped. Horrified, she quickly realized that this must have been caught on a security camera inside the Dane apartment.

As Nicole continued to watch, a small Asian woman, who she guessed was the maid, rushed forward in an effort to keep them out. When one of the men hit her in the face with his gun, Nicole moaned. The violence was too remi-niscent of what she'd lived through. Sick to her stomach, she fisted her hands against her belly, wishing it was over, but unable to tear her gaze away.

When the maid dropped to the carpet, the same man followed with a vicious kick to the little woman's mid-section that lifted her off the floor.

"Oh, my God," Nicole said. When blood began to pool beneath the maid's head, she started to cry.

As the tape played on, the four men split up in different directions. The camera caught one running down a long marble hallway, then disappearing into a room. Moments later he reappeared, carrying a little girl, who Nicole assumed was Molly Dane. The child was wearing a pair of red pants and a white turtleneck sweater, and her hair was partially blocking her abductor's face as he carried her down the hall. She was kicking and screaming in his arms, and when he slapped her, it elicited an agonized scream that brought the other three running. Nicole watched in horror as one of them ran up and put his hand over Molly's face. Seconds later, she went limp.

One moment they were in the foyer, then they were gone.

Nicole jumped to her feet, then staggered drunkenly. The bowl of ice cream she'd absentmindedly placed in her lap shattered at her feet, splattering glass and melting ice cream everywhere.

The picture on the screen abruptly switched from the kidnapping to what Nicole assumed was a rerun of Lyla Dane's plea for her daughter's safe return, but she was numb.

Before she could think what to do next, the doorbell rang. Startled by the unexpected sound, she shakily swiped at the tears and took a step forward. She didn't feel the glass shards piercing her feet until she took the second step. At that point, sharp pains shot through her foot. She gasped, then looked down in confusion. Her legs looked as if she'd been running through mud, and she was standing in broken glass and ice cream, while a thin ribbon of blood seeped out from beneath her toes.

"Oh, no," Nicole mumbled, then stifled a second moan of pain.

The doorbell rang again. She shivered, then clutched her head in confusion.

"Just a minute!" she yelled, then tried to sidestep the rest of the debris as she hobbled to the door.

When she looked through the peephole in the door, she didn't know whether to be relieved or regretful.

It was Dominic, and as usual, she was a mess.

Nicole smiled a little self-consciously as she opened the door to let him in. "I just don't know what's happening to me. I think I'm losing my mind."

"Hey, don't talk about my woman like that."

Nicole rode the surge of delight his words brought. "So I'm still your woman?"

Dominic lowered his head.

Their lips met.

The kiss proceeded.

Slowly.

Thoroughly.

* * * * *

Be sure to look for the
AFTERSHOCK *anthology next month,*
as well as other exciting paranormal stories
from Silhouette Nocturne.
Available in October wherever books are sold.

nocturne™

NEW YORK TIMES BESTSELLING AUTHOR

SHARON SALA

JANIS REAMES HUDSON
DEBRA COWAN

AFTERSHOCK

Three women are brought to the brink of death...
only to discover the aftershock of their trauma has
left them with unexpected and unwelcome gifts of
paranormal powers. Now each woman must learn to
accept her newfound abilities while fighting for life,
love and second chances....

Available October wherever books are sold.

www.eHarlequin.com
www.paranormalromanceblog.wordpress.com
SN61796

SPECIAL EDITION™

BRAVO FAMILY TIES

Tanner Bravo and Crystal Cerise had it bad
for each other, though they couldn't be more
different. Tanner was the type to settle down;
free-spirited Crystal wouldn't hear of it.
Now that Crystal was pregnant, would
Tanner have his way after all?

Look for

HAVING
TANNER BRAVO'S
BABY

by *USA TODAY* bestselling author
CHRISTINE RIMMER

Available in October wherever books are sold.

REQUEST YOUR FREE BOOKS!

2 FREE NOVELS
PLUS 2
FREE GIFTS!

Silhouette® Desire®

Passionate, Powerful, Provocative!

YES! Please send me 2 FREE Silhouette Desire® novels and my 2 FREE gifts (gifts are worth about $10). After receiving them, if I don't wish to receive any more books, I can return the shipping statement marked "cancel". If I don't cancel, I will receive 6 brand-new novels every month and be billed just $4.05 per book in the U.S. or $4.74 per book in Canada, plus 25¢ shipping and handling per book and applicable taxes, if any*. That's a savings of almost 15% off the cover price! I understand that accepting the 2 free books and gifts places me under no obligation to buy anything. I can always return a shipment and cancel at any time. Even if I never buy another book, the two free books and gifts are mine to keep forever.

225 SDN ERVX 326 SDN ERVM

Name	(PLEASE PRINT)
Address	Apt. #
City	State/Prov.	Zip/Postal Code

Signature (if under 18, a parent or guardian must sign)

Mail to the Silhouette Reader Service:
IN U.S.A.: P.O. Box 1867, Buffalo, NY 14240-1867
IN CANADA: P.O. Box 609, Fort Erie, Ontario L2A 5X3

Not valid to current subscribers of Silhouette Desire books.

Want to try two free books from another line?
Call 1-800-873-8635 or visit www.morefreebooks.com.

* Terms and prices subject to change without notice. N.Y. residents add applicable sales tax. Canadian residents will be charged applicable provincial taxes and GST. Offer not valid in Quebec. This offer is limited to one order per household. All orders subject to approval. Credit or debit balances in a customer's account(s) may be offset by any other outstanding balance owed by or to the customer. Please allow 4 to 6 weeks for delivery. Offer available while quantities last.

Your Privacy: Silhouette Books is committed to protecting your privacy. Our Privacy Policy is available online at www.eHarlequin.com or upon request from the Reader Service. From time to time we make our lists of customers available to reputable third parties who may have a product or service of interest to you. If you would prefer we not share your name and address, please check here. ☐

SDES08R

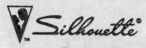

COMING NEXT MONTH

#1897 MARRIAGE, MANHATTAN STYLE—Barbara Dunlop
Park Avenue Scandals
Secrets, blackmail and infertility had their marriage on the rocks. Will an unexpected opportunity at parenthood give them a second chance?

#1898 THE MONEY MAN'S SEDUCTION—Leslie LaFoy
Gifts from a Billionaire
Suspicious of her true motives, he vows to keep her close—but as close as in his bed?

#1899 DANTE'S CONTRACT MARRIAGE—Day Leclaire
The Dante Legacy
Forced to marry to protect an infamous diamond, they never counted on being struck by The Dante Inferno. Suddenly their convenient marriage is full of *in*convenient passion.

#1900 AN AFFAIR WITH THE PRINCESS—Michelle Celmer
Royal Seductions
He'd had an affair with the princess, once upon a time. But why had he returned? Remembrance…or revenge?

#1901 MISTAKEN MISTRESS—Tessa Radley
The Saxon Brides
Could this woman he feels such a reckless passion for really be his late brother's mistress? Or are there other secrets she's hiding?

#1902 BABY BENEFITS—Emily McKay
Billionaires and Babies
Her boss had a baby—and he needed her help. How could she possibly deny him…how could she ever resist him?

SDCNM0908